# A Dark and Devious Tail
## A Sassy Sarcastic Cat Cozy Mystery

Rachel Woods

BonzaiMoon Books LLC
Houston, Texas
www.bonzaimoonbooks.com

This is a work of fiction. Names, characters, places and incidents either are the product of the authors' imaginations or are used fictitiously, and any resemblance to actual persons, living or dead, business establishments, events, or locales is entirely coincidental.

# Hey, y'all, hey!!!

Subscribe to my newsletter and you'll get inspiring rescue stories, hilarious cat memes, and thrilling serialized fiction. Plus, you can find out first about new books featuring my fabulous life as a feisty, fierce feline, and much more!

**Sign me up!**

*Sassy Callie*

https://subscribepage.io/SassyCallie

# Prologue

My name is Sophie Carter, I'm a junior reporter for the *Palmchat Gazette,* and I have a talking cat.

Now, if I was playing that game, Two Truths and a Lie, the lie would, of course, be that I have a talking cat. Because I don't.

Callie, the Calico cat who talks to me—meaning, I can understand everything she says as though she's speaking English and she can understand everything I say to her, as though I'm speaking cat or feline—is *not* my cat. I have to make that very clear, or Callie will scratch my eyes right out of my head. So, I don't have a talking cat, which technically makes my declaration about having a talking cat a lie.

The truth is that I know a cat who talks to me.

Callie the Calico.

And talking to me is not the only thing she does. For the past few months, Callie has been helping me solve mysteries as I investigate crime stories for the newspaper where I work. To hear Callie tell it— and you probably wouldn't hear her tell you, unless you understand feline, which I'm assuming you don't—the only reason that I've solved several cases is because of her. That's not exactly true but she has been extremely instrumental in helping me clear my name when I was accused of murder, expose shady diamond thieves, and rescue a Corgi who'd been dognapped.

My successful sleuthing has resulted in me keeping my job at the paper, which was on the line due to the fact that, technically, I'm a lifestyle reporter, not an investigative reporter focusing on crime—yet. My boss continues to promise that he'll ship me out if I don't shape up. I'm happy to report that I haven't been shipped out, so far. With Callie helping me fight crime and corruption in St. Mateo, the beautiful Caribbean island where we live, I think I'll keep my byline.

Because my goal is to become an investigative reporter, one of the things I'm currently working on is helping Callie find out more about her past. Callie doesn't know who she belongs to or where she came from. She has a condition called selective catnesia, a feline form of selective amnesia. Meaning, some things she remembers, and some things she doesn't—like how she ended up trapped in a Seagrape tree, which is where I found her.

To date, I haven't made much progress in finding out more about Callie's past.

I've come close, but my leads have all led nowhere. Each time I think I have answers, I end up with more questions. Recently, I thought I had a viable clue after I discovered Callie was abandoned in the bathroom at a coffee shop. Unfortunately, the barista who found Callie knew nothing about the person who'd left her there.

So, we're back to square one with the investigation into Callie's former life.

Not that I mind being back at square one.

Of course, I want to give Callie the answers about her life that she's hoping for, but when I learn the truth, it might be a tough pill for me to swallow. Especially if Callie has to go back to the humans she belongs to …

But I try not to think about that.

Instead, lately, I've been thinking about how I'm able to understand Callie.

The secret may have something to do with the fact that, after I rescued Callie from the Seagrape tree, she attacked me. She bit me so viciously that the wound became infected, and I fell into a coma. Three days later, when I regained consciousness, the Calico and I could speak to each other.

But I'm not sure.

Honestly, there are days when I'm still not certain that Callie and I do understand each other. Days when I think the coma did something strange to my mind. Maybe I'm suffering the effects of an odd psychosis which makes me believe I can communicate with the fierce feline.

I want to know for sure, of course.

I need more information, though.

The detailed, details.

Until then …

# Chapter 1

Normally, on a humid, overcast day with the potential for afternoon thunderstorms, I would spend the morning at my desk in my cubicle at the *Palmchat Gazette*, the newspaper where I'm a junior reporter, listening to the online police scanner for the St. Mateo Police Department while eating cinnamon-honey glazed donut holes and drinking honey-infused green tea.

But at eight-something a.m., I'm not doing that.

Instead, I'm having a meeting with my boss Marty, the editor of the St. Mateo division of the *Palmchat Gazette*. I must say, I think things are going well. I don't want to get the cart before the goat, of course, but Marty seems less frustrated with me, but not by much. The good news is his face isn't as red as it normally is when he admonishes me. Usually, his skin is as flushed as a steamed lobster or a crushed tomato or a ripe strawberry or … well, as red as any number of very red things. But his cheeks aren't particularly inflamed. Instead, there are small patches of pale pink dotting his skin. I can't read too much into that, though. He's still scowling. And his yellow, thin, straw-like hair still stands on his scalp like broken bristles from an old-fashioned house broom.

It's entirely possible that he's livid with me.

Or, if not livid then annoyed.

Or, if not annoyed, then—

"First of all, Sophia, in the interest of providing positive feedback," begins Marty as he paces around his desk, squeezing a stress ball, which is something he only seems to do when he's talking to me. I'm not quite sure why, though. I don't consider myself particularly stressful. That is, I don't think I cause people to become stressed out. Now, full disclosure, I suppose I can be frustrating, at times. And possibly irritating. But I don't think I'm—

"You did a decent job on the story about the actress's kidnapped dog."

Delighted by the praise, I smile as brightly as the mint-and-fuchsia striped wrap dress I'm wearing.

"Oh, I'm so glad you think so!" I exclaim. "I was hoping you would. I certainly tried my best!"

"Your story trended for weeks. Got lots of engagement. A ton of subscribers. And, most importantly, more advertisers."

"It was a rather riveting story," I say, deciding to toot my own horn a bit. "That poor dog went through so much. I was happy I could rescue him."

"Your involvement in solving the case helped the story go viral," Marty says. "I have to commend you on that."

"Thanks so much!" I say, resisting the urge to squeal with amazement. I'm not very sure how to think about Marty's compliments. He's never liked any of my stories. He's told me on numerous occasions that I shouldn't be an investigative reporter. Technically, I'm supposed to cover lifestyle stories—basically, articles tourists would find interesting, things like highlighting unique attractions, local cultures, and off-the-beaten-path experiences travelers can enjoy.

And while I do like writing about eco-friendly resorts, traditional

Caribbean dishes, and the literary contributions of Caribbean writers and poets, my true interest lies in crooks and corruption, mayhem and murder. My goal is to become a great investigative reporter.

Although I've done crime reporting in the past, Marty remains reluctant to allow me the chance to cover the crime beat. He claims that I don't have "it." And, for clarity's sake, "it," according to Marty, is experience. Specifically, decades of investigating and writing about crime. Which, since I'm only twenty-three and graduated from university two years ago, I don't have.

Nevertheless, I've been trying to get lots of experience investigating and writing about crime so that I can convince Marty that I have "it." If I can't convince Marty that I'm a good crime reporter, he's threatened to ship me out if I don't shape up. And by "shape up," he means to focus on my lifestyle stories and forget about covering crime, even though he knows crime is what I want to cover.

And he doesn't care that I wrote crime stories at the *Palmchat Gazette*'s main headquarters in St. Killian. Or that I was regularly assigned crime stories by Vivian Thomas-Bronson.

In addition to being the wife of the paper's publisher, Vivian is also an award-winning, world-renowned journalist best known for her in-depth, hard-hitting, intelligent work as a foreign war correspondent. While reporting on atrocities in the South Sudan, she uncovered rampant crime and corruption. Naturally, I aspire to have a career as esteemed as hers.

"But don't get too excited, Sophia," warns Marty.

"Don't get too excited about what?"

"The positive feedback."

"But why shouldn't I?" I ask, confused. "It is exciting."

"What I mean is," says Marty, "that, because of your lack of experience, you still need lots of improvement."

"Oh," I say, deflating a bit. "Well, yes, I'm sure I do, but—"

"Your crime reporting was less atrocious," Marty says, tossing the stress ball into the air with one hand and catching it with the other.

"Less atrocious," I say, tilting my head as I stare at him. "Meaning, good?"

"I wouldn't go that far, Sophia," Marty says.

"Well, how far would you go?" I ask.

Rolling his eyes, Marty says, "Not far enough."

"I don't understand."

"The way you investigate crime isn't great," says Marty. "But it's not bad. You seem to be getting … less terrible at covering crime."

"Less terrible," I say. "Meaning—"

"Meaning I'm giving you another chance to impress me," says Marty. "Another chance to not annoy me or irritate me with your lack of experience."

"I need to impress, but not annoy or irritate," I say. "Hmmm. Well, hopefully, I have a goat of a chance to do that."

Glaring at me, Marty says. "Don't you mean a ghost of a chance?"

"No, I mean a goat of a chance."

"Wait a minute," says Marty. "We had this conversation before, didn't we?"

"Possibly," I say, trying to remember.

"Whatever. Anyway." Marty scowls, then says, "There's a story I want you to cover."

"What's it about?" I ask, excited.

"Dead body found on the beach," Marty says. "Appears a swarm of bees stung the victim to death."

# Chapter 2

"Hey, girl, hey!" Callie calls out.

Walking across the *Palmchat Gazette* toward my vehicle, I wave at the Calico. As always, I'm super happy to see the fierce feline, even though she's not my cat. However, I am her human. For now, anyway, I suppose. The selective catnesia robbed Callie of certain memories about her past, namely who she really belongs to. Callie has no idea who her real human is, so I'm helping her find out where she came from.

One of the things that's always concerned me is how I found Callie.

She was trapped in one of the Seagrape trees bordering the parking lot, meowing in pain. The way she was tangled in the tree seemed, to me, at least, deliberate. That is, I'm not certain Callie got caught in the tree by herself. I've always wondered if someone put her in the tree, but why would they do that? I don't know. And Callie doesn't, either. That is, she doesn't know how she ended up in the tree.

Nevertheless, I'm committed to finding out the truth about Callie's past and giving her the answers, even if it means giving her up. Technically, that shouldn't be hard to do because, officially, she's not my cat. Still, in my heart, she does belong to me. I want her in my life forever, but if that's not to be, then I'm thankful I'll have memories to cherish.

"Where're you headed?" asks the cat, licking her paw as she sits on the hood of my red JEEP, her usual place to wait for me.

"Marty gave me a new assignment," I say. "A dead body was discovered on Golden beach this morning."

Callie looks at me. "What happened?"

"Not really sure," I say, opening the driver's side door. "Marty said the victim had been stung to death by bees."

"Girl, are you serious?" Callie goes back to licking her paw. "That's horrible. But you have to be careful around bees. If they feel threatened, they'll ... well, sting you to death."

"So, I'm off to get the detailed details," I say. "Want to come along?"

"Why not?" says Callie as she jumps from the hood to the top of the door frame, and then leaps down into the JEEP, ambling over the cup holder and settling into the passenger's seat. "I don't have anything better to do."

Twenty minutes later, I'm trudging along the beach, trying to walk on the powdery white sand in wedge heels.

Trotting next to me, Callie says, "Girl, you've got the wrong shoes on."

"Tell me about it," I say, glancing ahead where a cluster of St. Mateo cops are gathered near a sand dune.

"You should take them off," Callie says. "The sand feels nice. Not too hot."

"Because it's still overcast," I say, looking up at the low deck of swirling gray clouds. "But I don't want to take my shoes off because I don't want sand between my toes."

"Girl, don't knock it until you've tried it," says Callie.

"Since you put it that way," I say, then stop to remove my left shoe, and then my right one.

"There's Officer Good-Looking," Callie says, taking off across the sand before I can stop her, heading in the direction of Officer Noah Cuetee, my secret unofficial confidential source at the St. Mateo police department.

"Wait up!" I call to the cat as I hurry after her. Not that I blame her for running toward Noah. He is very good-looking. The kind of guy my grandma would describe as a dreamboat. I'll confess to having a slight crush on him, and I think he likes me, too. Maybe. But we haven't gone on any dates or anything. This is not to say that I wouldn't like to date him, because I would. It's just that I don't have time for romance right now. I'm too busy working on my career. Trying to get "it" so I can accomplish my goal of being a great investigative reporter.

Falling in love would be a distraction.

As I approach Officer Cuetee, he breaks away from the circle of policemen he'd been conversing with. Walking toward me, cradling Callie, he smiles. I'm not surprised to see the calico snuggling in his arms.

"Well, well, well," I say, stopping in front of Officer Cuetee, giving Callie a playful side-eye. "What do we have here? Seems she likes you."

"Don't hate, sis," Callie advises.

"I'm not hating," I tell the cat, reaching to scratch her head.

"Watch it, girl," Callie warns.

"You're not hating ... what?" Officer Cuetee asks.

Panicked, realizing my mistake, I look up at him. "Oh, um, well, you see ..."

"Girl, all that stuttering is not helping," Callie says.

"Obviously not," I mutter.

"Obviously not ... what?" asks Officer Cuetee.

"Oops, you did it again, girl," Callie says.

Yeah, it appears I did. Unfortunately, I do it a lot. Answer Callie while I'm talking to another person, that is. Because I'm the only human who can understand the cat, when I speak to her in front of someone, it's like a non-sequitur. Then people look at me strangely, and I'm at a loss for words because, really, there are no words. It's not like I can tell people that Callie talks to me, and I understand her.

Clearing my throat, I say, "So ... I got assigned to the dead body found on the beach. What can you tell me?"

"The victim is a middle-aged woman," says Officer Cuetee. "No identification was found on the body so we're not sure who she is, but CSI will run her prints and we might get a match. If not, we might need the *Palmchat Gazette* to run a sketch of her to see if someone knows who she is."

Nodding, I ask, "Do you know who found the body?"

"Three beach vendors," says Officer Cuetee, scratching beneath Callie's chin. "But Detective François hasn't arrived yet to question them."

"Which means you need to question them first, sis," says Callie. "Get the tea before they spill it all to that detective. You know he doesn't like you so he's not going to share any detailed details."

"You're right," I say. "Good idea."

Officer Cuetee gives me a half-frown, half-smile. "What's a good idea?"

"I want to talk to the beach vendors," I tell Officer Cuetee, ignoring his question, despite my slip-up. "Where are they?"

"Set up over near the snack stand," he says, as Callie leaps down from his arms.

Glancing over my shoulder, I look down the beach.

The snack stand, a wooden structure comprised of five stalls painted in pastel colors, sits in front of the paved pedestrian pathway separating the beach from the clusters of Seagrape and Palm trees. At almost nine in the morning, there are only a few people in line for food. From where I'm standing, I can just make out the side walls of the vendor tents.

"Come on, girl, let's go!" Callie says, taking off down the sand.

"Wait up!" I call to her before turning back to Officer Cuetee. "Thanks for the info."

"No problem," he says, smiling. "Hey, I forgot to mention … a new tea shop opened up near the marina."

"Really?" I say, enthralled by the idea of another quaint shop to enjoy my favorite libation. "What's it called?"

"T is for Tea," he says.

"How cute!"

"I thought we might give it a try this weekend," suggests Officer Cuetee.

Giving him a bright smile, I say, "Absolutely!"

# Chapter 3

"Excuse me …?" I say to a trio of women huddled beneath a tent overflowing with hundreds of kitschy bric-a-bracs laid across three tables positioned to form a U.

Each piece is made from either shells, starfish, or sand.

In fact, that's the name of the vendor booth—Shells, Starfish, and Sand. The women standing in the center of the U seem as different and varied as shells are from starfish and as starfish is from sand.

"Is there anybody else you can talk to, sis?" asks Callie. "These beach bunnies look delulu."

Normally, I'm the last person to call someone crazy, because I don't have the knowledge to make such clinical assessments, but Callie might be right. After all, as she always tells me, cats know these things.

The women, who were heatedly debating some topic as I approached the tent, which was the only one occupied, turn and give me shrewd, appraising looks. The one on the right has salt-and-pepper dreadlocs and wears green army fatigues. The woman in the center wears a white, slinky ball gown with a fur stole and a tiara nestled in her bouncy, auburn curls. On the left is a cricket mom type in jeans and a T-shirt that says I love the Palmchat Islands.

"What kind of reading you need, sweetie?" demands the cricket mom.

"What kind of ... reading?" I repeat, confused.

"Girl, why are they talking about reading?" Callie asks, jumping up onto one of the tables. "I don't see any books. All I see is a bunch of junk."

Exhaling and rolling her eyes, the woman wearing the tiara asks, "Shell reading, starfish reading, or sand reading?"

"Oh," I say, understanding the service they provide, which is just a tourist trap. Lots of locals set up stands on the beach, claiming they can read futures and fortunes with shells, tentacles, barnacles, sea oat grass, driftwood, and any number of other items that wash ashore.

It's all mumbo-jumbo, but the scam is lucrative, especially on days when the cruise ships dock in the harbor and the beach is teeming with gullible passengers.

Shaking my head, I say, "I don't need a shell, starfish, or sand reading."

"So they're not crazy," says Callie, licking her paw. "They're grifters."

"I have a question," I say.

"About your future?" asks the woman in green fatigues.

"Or about the man you're going to marry?" asks the woman wearing the tiara.

"Or about whether or not you'll win big at the goat races?" asks the cricket mom.

"No, no, and no," I say, even though I wouldn't mind knowing if the goat I put money on will win big. "I'm wondering if you three found the dead body on the beach this morning?"

Nodding in the affirmative, they confess to finding the woman who'd been stung to death, talking over and around and in between each other as they explain how they'd been looking for shells and sand and starfish near the bushes further down the beach.

"And then there the body was," says the woman in green fatigues. "Covered in bees! They were all over her face and hands! Just gruesome!"

"She was lying near a hibiscus tree," the woman wearing a tiara says.

"Dressed in what looked like, to me, at least, scrubs," says the cricket mom.

"Dressed in scrubs?" I echo.

"Was the victim dressed in scrubs?" asks Callie, licking her foot.

I glance at her, giving a quick nod.

"But they were of a nicer fabric," says the woman in green fatigues.

"Like fancy scrubs," says the woman in the tiara.

"Sort of like the ones the employees wear in those expensive, luxury spas," says cricket mom.

"So … maybe the victim worked in a spa," I say.

"Possibly," says the woman in green fatigues.

"Well … wouldn't you know?" I ask.

"How would we know?"

"Wouldn't the shells or the starfish or the sand tell you something about the woman?" I ask.

"Good question, sis," says Callie. "They should know the woman's name, age, and Palmchat Islands ID number."

"Sweetie, that's not how it works."

"How does it work then?"

"The shells and sand and starfish provide the answers they think we should know," says the woman in the tiara. "We don't demand answers from them."

"But that doesn't mean the sand didn't reveal some things about this horrible situation," says the woman in green fatigues.

Cricket mom says, "The shells had something to say, as well."

"And so did the starfish."

Dubious, I try to keep the doubt from my voice when I ask, "Is that so?"

"Girl, what are they talking about?" Callie asks. And not because she's confused. But because she can't understand what the women are saying. Callie can't understand what any other humans are saying. I'm the only person she can communicate with, which is odd because she's explained to me that all animals can understand humans, even though humans can't understand animals.

Glancing at Callie, I say, "The shells, sand, and starfish revealed something about the dead woman you found on the beach, is that what you expect me to believe?"

"Girl, I told you they were delulu," says Callie.

"Believe it, or not," says the cricket mom, her eyes widening as she stares at me. "But the shells exposed the motive for the bee attack. The dead woman was stealing their honey. It was a revenge killing."

"That's not true," says the woman in the tiara. "According to the starfish, she was trying to stop them from making honey ... she's allergic and hates bees and wants to wipe all bees from the face of the earth. So, the bees had no choice but to get rid of her first."

"That's preposterous!" exclaims the woman in green fatigues. "The dead woman wanted them to make a specific type of honey and the bees promised her they would but they got her order wrong, and she got very upset and tried to kill them so they had no choice but to defend themselves."

"I see ..." I say, realizing Callie was right. These women are quite wacky. "Okay, well—"

"Uh oh, sis," Callie stands, her ears erect, and facing sideways. "Here comes trouble."

Before I can figure out what Callie means, I feel a heavy tapping against my shoulder, pressing it down.

The women stare at whoever's behind me, their expressions curious, attentive, and appreciative.

Worried, I turn.

Detective Richland François glares at me. Immediately, I feel myself wilting, and not from the damp humidity. The detective is tall, muscular, handsome, and completely adverse to the press. He never gives me a statement, even though I always ask. It's always 'no comment' and a threat to stay out of his investigation.

Swallowing, I take a step back and try to smile. "Oh, um, hi—"

"What are you doing?" the detective demands.

"What am I doing?" I squeak. "Well, you see, I was, um—"

"Girl, don't let him bully you," Callie says. "You have a right to investigate this case. Show him your press pass."

"Yes, right ..." I mutter, unzipping my crossbody purse.

"Ms. Carter, I asked you a question."

"And I'm trying to answer," I say, tugging on the zipper, which seems to be fighting against me, refusing to open. "I'm getting my press pass because—"

"I don't care about your press pass," the detective tells me. "I need to question these witnesses. And you need to leave."

"Right, yes," I say, attempting yet another smile that doesn't quite make it to the corner of my lips. "Well ... good luck!"

Minutes later, as Callie and I head back down the beach, I say, "Marty's going to kill me. I forgot to ask Detective François for a statement."

"Well, you're not any more forgetful than I am," says the feline.

"What do you mean?"

"I forgot to scratch his eyes right out of his head!"

# Chapter 4

"Bees didn't kill the dead woman those kooks found on the beach," says Callie, settling herself in the grass near my feet.

It's a lovely day in the tropics, picture perfect with azure skies, and a gentle, salty breeze that rustles the fronds on the Palm trees at the Golden Beach dog park. I'm sitting on a bench, waiting for Officer Cuetee who agreed to meet me here for lunch. While his K-9 partner, Dutiful, a faithful, fierce Belgian Malinois runs around with the other dogs, Officer Cuetee and I plan to coordinate our upcoming trip to T is for Tea, the new tea café.

"What makes you think that?" I ask the cat.

Three days have passed since the body was found. After Detective François ran me off the beach, I dropped Callie off at a small boutique hotel that has a cat colony and then drove back to work. My article, UNKNOWN WOMAN STUNG TO DEATH AT GOLDEN BEACH comprised the basic facts known at the time. Marty didn't love it but said it was "more okay" than he thought it would be, although he seemed reluctant to admit this. When Officer Cuetee shows up, I'm hoping he'll have more information so I can give my readers the detailed details of the case.

"Remember my friend, BB?" asks Callie, rising to her feet.

"You mean the honeybee who tried to sting me?"

"BB wasn't trying to sting you," Callie says, leaping up onto the bench. "She was trying to give you the tea. Just like she gave me the tea about the body on the beach."

"What did she say?"

"Remember how the kooks told you the body was covered in bees?"

Shuddering at the gruesome memory, I nod. "So terrible. What she must have suffered!"

"Well, that's just it, sis," says Callie. "She didn't suffer."

"How can you say she didn't suffer?" I ask. "All those bee stings!"

"There were no bee stings," says the feline.

I narrow my eyes at her. "What do you mean? How was she stung to death by bees if there were no bee stings?"

"Because the bees didn't sting her," says Callie. "According to BB, those bees were dead."

Nodding, I say, "Yes, because bees die after they sting a person."

Callie says, "No, because those bees had been dead for months and were placed on the dead body to make it look like they stung the woman to death."

"What?" I'm shocked. "Are you serious? How does BB know—"

"Talking to your cat again?"

Jumping, I look over my shoulder.

Officer Cuetee and Dutiful are standing a few feet away from the bench.

Dutiful barks.

Licking her paw, Callies says, "I'm much better than you, Dutiful. I don't have to wear a leash. You want to know why? Because cats can't be tamed."

Dutiful barks again.

Callie says, "I don't care if Benny the Bengal wears a leash. He's a police station mascot cat. I don't expect a feline with a government job to be independent."

"Wonder what they're carrying on about?" asks Officer Cuetee, taking a seat next to me on the bench while Dutiful lays in the grass.

Giggling, I say, "Callie is throwing shade because she doesn't have to wear a leash."

"It's not shade, girl," the cat tells me. "It's facts."

Frowning, Officer Cuetee asks, "And how do you know that?"

"Oh, I actually don't know that," I say, mentally kicking myself. "I was just, you know, imagining what the conversation might be like. Anyway, um … I wanted to ask you if there are any new developments in the bee sting case."

"As a matter of fact," says Officer Cuetee, "There have been some strange developments."

"Strange how?" I ask.

"Well, initially we thought the victim was stung to death by bees because they were all over her body," he says, frowning. "But, as it turned out, according to the forensic pathologist, there was no evidence that she was stung."

Dutiful barks a few times.

"Girl, didn't I tell you that bees didn't kill that woman?" asks Callie.

Shocked, I lean over and pretend to scratch my ankle. Whispering to the cat, I ask, "Did you understand Officer Cuetee?"

Whispering back, Callie says, "No, sis … Dutiful is translating for me so you're off the hook. But, don't respond to me because the dufus doggo can't know that I understand you."

"Sophie … you okay?" asks Officer Cuetee.

Sitting up, I angle toward him. "I think something bit my ankle. Yes, so … that is strange. If she wasn't stung to death, then how did she die?"

"We're not sure," says Officer Cuetee. "There was a high concentration of bee venom in her blood."

Dutiful barks a few times.

"Calm down, boy," Officer Cuetee tells the dog. "I'll take you to the park in a second."

"Interesting …" says Callie to the Belgian Malinois. "How did she get bee venom in her blood?"

"Good question …" I say.

"I didn't ask a question," Officer Cuetee says.

"Oh, no, of course not, um …" I clear my throat. "I meant, a good question would be … how did the victim get bee venom in her blood?"

"Detective François has a theory," says Officer Cuetee. "The victim was Dora Butler. A forty-three-year-old nurse who worked at a medical spa that features honeybee products."

Dutiful barks, translating for Callie.

"We're going, boy," says Officer Cuetee, trying to calm Dutiful, even though he doesn't have to, but I can't tell him that his dog is talking to my cat … who isn't really my cat, just a cat I know.

"A nurse at a med spa," Callie says to Dutiful. "That explains the nice scrubs."

"What's François' theory?" I ask.

"He thinks she might have accidentally poisoned herself."

# Chapter 5

"Girl, you really think the victim poisoned herself?" asks Callie as I pull into a space in the *Palmchat Gazette* parking lot.

After shifting to Park, I cut the JEEP's ignition and glance at the Calico.

"Well, I suppose it's possible," I say. "If the nurse worked with bees in order to administer products made with beeswax, then she might have extracted bee venom. Maybe."

Callie gives me a scathing side-eye. "Whatever, sis. I don't believe that, and you shouldn't, either. It makes no sense. Why would she be extracting venom from bees?"

"I'm not sure," I say, biting my lower lip. "It's odd, but ... maybe the medical spa was using bee venom in one of their treatments. After all, spas do those vampire facials where they withdraw the person's blood and inject it into their face."

Licking her paw, Callie says, "Girl, just when I think you humans might have some sense, I realize that I was wrong."

Giggling, I say, "Well ... we try to be sensible."

"Not hard enough," says Callie, rising to all fours. "Anyway, sis, I gotta go."

"Where are you headed?" I ask, reaching over to open the passenger door.

"Not that it's any of your business," she says, "but the tomcat is taking me to lunch."

"Oh!" I say, clapping my hands. "A date?"

"Girl, he thinks so," says Callie.

"And what do you think?"

Callie gives me a look. "I think he better not try to recreate a *Lady and the Tramp* moment because he's been hanging out behind an Italian restaurant."

"But that would be so romantic," I say, thinking of the iconic scene. "You and Tom start to eat the same spaghetti noodle, coming closer together until you end up in an accidental but delightfully surprising kiss!"

"If Tom wants to recreate a Disney scene, he needs to pick something from the *Aristocats*," Callie says. "Do I look like a canine?"

And with that, Callie leaps out of the JEEP and scampers away.

Moments later, at my desk, I decide to research the victim, Dora Butler, the medical spa nurse. With the updated information Officer Cuetee gave me, I have to write a follow-up story. Adding details about the victim will enhance the article and give readers a chance to know Dora Butler as more than a body found on the beach.

After locating her personal information from the online database the paper subscribes to in order to do background checks, I make notes, then move on to researching her former place of employment —the Bee Well Medical Center.

Turns out, according to the website, it's an exclusive, luxury facility focused on providing holistic skin care therapy through the use of products from bees. Located on a small outlying island that can only be reached by private ferry, the spa boasts its very own apiary where dedicated beekeepers maintain and care for the hives. Beeswax, pollen, and honey are used to make skin serums, cleaners, toners, and moisturizers which promise to turn back the hands of time. The founder of the medical center, Dr. Ricardo Napier, claims to have created products that have the same effect as a fountain of youth.

I read through dozens of testimonials from satisfied clients who are overjoyed by their results. There are corresponding before and after photos that absolutely attest to the doctor's bold claims. The women featured appear to have walked into the medical center as fifty-somethings and left looking twenty-nine.

"Wow ..." I whisper, wondering if I need a pollen-infused serum. At twenty-three, I don't have any fine lines or wrinkles, but I suppose it's never too early to take care of your skin. Which I absolutely do. My regimen consists of double cleansing, followed by—

"Better not let Marty catch you goofing off on the internet ..."

Recognizing the deep voice, I swivel in my chair to face my friend and coworker, Clark Kent. And yes, that's his real name. And, again, yes, he does look like Superman.

"I'm not goofing off," I protest, smiling at Clark, because it's kind of hard not to. He's so cute. "I'm researching my bee sting death story."

Leaning down toward me, Clark peers at my computer screen. "Research? Looks like you're about to book an appointment at a spa."

Rolling my eyes good-naturedly, I turn back to the computer. "Actually, I can't book an appointment at this place. The Bee Well Medical Center is by invitation only from a referral."

"What does that place have to do with your story?"

"The victim, Dora Butler, worked there as a nurse," I say, then swivel to face Clark again.

"Was she stung by bees from the facility?"

Shaking my head, I say, "Actually, despite the high levels of bee venom in her blood, she wasn't stung to death by bees."

"So how did she die?"

"Officer Cuetee told me—"

Clark laughs out loud.

Confused, I stare at him. "Something funny?"

"Your boyfriend's name," says Clark. "Officer *Cuetee*."

"First of all, he's not my boyfriend," I say, crossing my arms over my chest. "And second … Officer Cuetee is about as funny as … Clark Kent."

"Ha ha," says Clark, looking sheepish. "So, what did he tell you?"

"Detective François thinks the victim accidentally poisoned herself with the bee venom," I say.

"How would she have done that?"

"That's what I have to find out," I say. "I figured I'd call the medical center and see if someone will talk to me."

"Well, I've got an assignment to get to, so I'll get out of your hair," says Clark.

"See ya," I say, giving him a little wave before I turn back to my computer.

"Oh, and Sophie …"

Glancing over my shoulder, I say, "Yeah?"

"You don't need to go to a facial spa," Clark says. "You'd be wasting your money."

Seconds after Clark leaves, I'm pondering his statement, wondering what he meant, wondering if he meant what I think he meant, wondering why I'm wondering when I need to call the spa.

Grabbing the receiver from my desk phone, I punch in the spa's number.

A few rings later I'm greeted by a pleasant, harmonic female voice. "Bee Well Medical Spa. This is Agnes, how may I assist you?"

After introducing myself, I state my business. "I'm working on the story about Dora Butler's death, and—"

"Ms. Carter, the Bee Well Medical Spa has no comment at this time," says Agnes. "We have already spoken to authorities, and—"

"What did you tell the police?"

Following a moment's hesitation, Agnes says, "I'm afraid—"

"Don't be afraid," I blurt out, not quite sure how I'm going to get the receptionist to talk to me, but knowing I have to, knowing it's what Callie would tell me to do.

"I'm sorry?"

"You were about to say you were afraid," I tell her. "And I was saying you shouldn't be."

"I'm not scared," Agnes clarifies. "I was going to say that I'm afraid I can't speak with you about this matter."

"Didn't you say the spa had already talked to the police?"

"That's correct," she says. "Our representative was questioned and gave a statement."

"Can't you tell me what your rep told the cops?"

"I'm sorry, I'm not authorized to—"

"Right, I understand," I say, feeling both desperate and bold. "But don't worry about me quoting you. My information can come from an anonymous source."

"My bosses might suspect that I'm the anonymous source," counters Agnes.

Drumming my nails against my desk, I say, "Yes, that's true … however, if you tell me what the rep told the police, I'll fact-check that information with the cops and when they verify it, I'll say I got my information from the police, which technically, will be true …"

There's silence on the other line.

A few more seconds pass.

Did she hang up on me?

"Agnes?"

Voice lowered, Agnes says, "I'm only telling you this—and I don't want my name in the paper, and I don't want to be called an anonymous source—because what Dora did was horrible!"

Confused, I ask, "Dora ending up dead on a beach was horrible?

Wait. Of course, it was. That's not how I meant to phrase that question—"

"What?" Agnes scoffs. "No, that wasn't horrible at all. That was what Dora deserved."

Now I really don't understand. "What do you mean?"

"Dora stole several colonies of bees from the apiary," Agnes says, her outrage evident in her tone.

"What?"

"And then she killed the bees, extracted their venom, and injected it into herself!"

"Wait. What?" I ask. "Are you serious?"

"Dora was a wrinkled old hag!" Agnes says. "She committed that heinous act, destroying hundreds of innocent bees, for no other reason than vanity!"

"Vanity?"

"She was trying to look younger!" Agnes says. "And it cost her her life."

# Chapter 6

"Girl, you really believe the nurse accidentally poisoned herself with bee venom so she could look younger?" asks Callie, licking her paw.

"Why wouldn't I?" I ask, opening a tube of mascara.

At ten o'clock on a rainy Saturday morning, I'm standing in my bathroom, peering at my face in the mirror, hoping I can achieve the look I want for my outing with Officer Cuetee at the new tea shop, T is for Tea. The Calico sits on the toilet lid. She showed up on my patio an hour ago, soaking wet from a mad dash to my apartment from God knows where—of course, she wouldn't tell me—so I got some fluffy towels to wrap around her.

Working together, we managed to get her from drenched to damp, then made our way into the bathroom where I blew her fur with my hair dryer.

"Because how does bee venom make you look younger?" Callie asks.

Shrugging, I pull the wand from the tube. "Well, she worked at a facility that specialized in making facial products from bees. Maybe the spa uses venom in one of its serums, but they only use a tiny amount. She might have thought using more venom would make her look younger much faster."

"Okay, let's say you're right," suggests the cat. "How do you explain the dead bees that were all over her body? You think she injected herself and then covered herself with bees? Girl, I know you humans lack basic common sense, but you're not that crazy."

Applying a coat of mascara to the lashes on my left eye, I frown at my reflection.

Callie does have a point. Dora Butler was covered with bees, which was why the first responders initially believed she'd been stung to death. But that wasn't the case.

"Officer Cuetee didn't mention the dead bees on Dora's body," I say, applying a few more coats. "But I'm sure François has a theory."

"Or maybe he doesn't," disputes Callie. "Maybe he's fine with thinking the victim accidentally poisoned herself to death, and he's closing the investigation."

"Well, it makes sense to close it because that's probably what happened," I say, blinking my left eye to determine the effect. Too much? Not enough? I'm not sure. "The receptionist at the medical spa told me that Dora Butler stole several bee hives. Why would she do that if she wasn't planning to extract venom and inject herself with it?"

"How do you know that's the reason Dora stole the bee hives?" challenges Callie, licking her foot. "How do you know she really stole the hives?"

"Why would the receptionist lie?" I ask, glancing at the Calico.

"Why would you automatically believe that the receptionist is telling the truth?" Callie asks. "Aren't you supposed to verify her version of events?"

Swiping the mascara wand across the lashes of my right eye, I say, "My job is to report the facts. I'm a reporter."

"Girl, you are trying to be an *investigative* reporter, last time I checked," says Callie. "That means you need to make sure the facts are actually the truth and not fake news."

Sighing, I stare at the cat. "You're right."

"Girl, I know I'm right."

"And you know, something you just said makes me wonder about something …"

"Wonder about what?"

"You asked me how bee venom could make someone look younger," I say, putting the mascara wand back into the tube. "And now that I'm remembering Dora Butler … she didn't look that old. Not from her Palmchat Islands driver's license, anyway. Of course, the photo might have been taken years earlier. I didn't check to see when the license was issued."

"Girl, you need to find out what Dora looked like before she died," Callie says.

Nodding, I pick up a tube of lip gloss. "The receptionist called her an old hag …"

"But, if she wasn't," says Callie. "Then I doubt she used bee venom to make herself look younger. And I doubt bee venom can get rid of fine lines and wrinkles, but I'll check with BB."

"When I go to work on Monday," I say, "I'll work on finding a current photo of Dora Butler."

Jumping down from the toilet lid, Callie settles near the edge of the claw-foot tub. "By the way, why are you trying to look cute? Or, rather, who are you trying to look cute for? You have a date?"

"Not a date," I say quickly, though I feel my cheeks warm. "Just going to check out a new tea shop with Officer Cuetee."

"Officer Cuetee," says the cat. "So, is it getting serious, sis? Tell me. You know cats are curious."

"It's about as serious as you and Tom Cat," I tell her, smirking.

The Calico gives me a look. "You like him, though, right?"

"About as much as you like the tomcat."

Callie hisses at me. "Well, I don't know if things are serious between you two and you won't tell me if you like him but at least now I understand the beat face."

"What do you know about a beat face?" I tease, wondering how the cat heard the term, a colloquial meaning for putting on glam makeup.

"What did I tell you, sis," Callie says. "Cats know things."

# Chapter 7

"The last time we talked, I forgot to ask you something," I say, adding orange-infused fig jam to my scone, which I wish was a donut hole, but T is for Tea doesn't offer donut holes.

The charming shop, decorated like a beach bungalow with pastels and bamboo furnishings, does provide a selection of baked scones, which do pair well with their teas. I'm having jasmine and lavender while, sitting across from me, Officer Cuetee enjoys mint and chai.

Even though the weather took an even sharper turn for the worst —it's raining nanny goats and billy goats, as my grandma would say —the vibe is laid back, like a lazy summer day.

"What's that?" asks Officer Cuetee, reaching for a papaya-glazed scone. He's dressed casually in a short-sleeved chambray shirt, khaki shorts, and deck shoes. And, not surprisingly, he's beyond handsome. An absolute dreamboat. Sitting at our table in the corner of the tea shop, I'm sure we look like we're on a date. Admittedly, part of me wishes we were, and maybe one day, we will go on a date, but I don't want to read too much into things. Right now, we're content to enjoy each other's company, which is fine with me. After all, I need to focus on my career. Can't afford to be distracted by love and romance and handsome guys.

"Dora Butler was found with dead bees all over her body, right?" I confirm, glancing at him.

Nodding, Officer Cuetee says, "Detective François is stumped about that detail, but he figures Dora Butler covered herself with bees in some bizarre beauty ritual."

"I spoke to the receptionist at the Bee Well spa," I say. "She told me that Dora Butler stole the beehives so she could extract venom from them and inject it into herself to look younger."

"That's what the spa rep told François," says Officer Cuetee. "And the story checks out. The medical spa reported the theft of the hives two days before Dora Butler was found dead."

"Interesting," I say, nibbling on the edge of my scone. "But I was thinking about Dora Butler trying to look younger."

"What about it?"

After another sip of tea, I say, "In Dora Butler's Palmchat Islands ID photo, she didn't look old."

Officer Cuetee shrugs. "Maybe it was an old photo you saw. Islanders have to get new ID's every ten years so you could have been looking at a thirty-three-year-old Dora Butler. You need a current photo."

Nodding, I say, "Yeah, that's what Callie said ..."

Chuckling softly, Officer Cuetee asks, "Callie? Your cat said that?"

Glancing away from his curious gaze, I clear my throat. "Oh, um, well, you see ... she's not my cat," I mumble, then grab a scone and shove it in my mouth before I say something else I shouldn't.

"Just a cat you know, right?"

Swallowing, I grab my teacup, but it's empty.

"Well, anyway, I was thinking about the bee venom," says Officer Cuetee. "And there is another use."

"What's that?" I ask.

"Arthritis," says Officer Cuetee.

"Really?" I ask. "I never knew that."

"Yeah, I looked it up," says Officer Cuetee. "There have been studies showing that people who used bee venom had fewer swollen joints, tender joints, and less morning stiffness than those who were given a placebo."

"Maybe Dora Butler was arthritic and trying to treat achy joints," I say.

"It's possible," says Officer Cuetee. "We'd have to get her medical records to make sure, though."

"Sad to think she accidentally poisoned herself trying to get rid of her pain," I say. "If that's what happened to her."

"Hey, speaking of that cat you know that's not your cat, did you ever find her owner?" asks Officer Cuetee.

"Unfortunately, no. So far, it's been nothing but dead ends," I lament, buttering another scone. "But, I have been wondering something ... "

Officer Cuetee grabs a croissant. "What's that?"

"How did Callie end up trapped in the seagrape tree?"

"Who knows?"

"I think I might be able to find out," I say. "Well, I'd need access to the CCTV cameras on the corner of the building across from the *Palmchat Gazette*. They point in the direction of the tree where I found Callie."

Giving me a sly smile, Officer Cuetee asks, "Are you asking me to try to access the cameras to see if they show someone leaving the cat in that seagrape tree?"

"Well, you know," I say, returning his teasing glance. "I wouldn't mind if you did."

Officer Cuetee says, "No promises, but I'll see what I can do. Just let me know the date and approximate time I need to check for."

"Will do. And thanks," I say, taking a sip of tea, feeling somewhat conflicted. Of course, I want to find out about Callie's past, where she came from and who she really belongs to, and I promised her I would.

But knowing who she is might mean giving her up.

And I'm not sure I can do that …

# Chapter 8

Coordinating with the *Palmchat Gazette's* Obituary Editor, I learn that Dora Butler's niece, her only living relative, arranged for her aunt's obituary to be featured in the paper.

Currently, on a quiet Monday morning, I'm at my desk in my cubicle scanning Dora's obit, looking at the photo, which was taken months ago and thus qualifies as current. Again, I'm struck by how much the woman doesn't look like an "old hag," as the Bee Well receptionist claimed.

Dora Butler looked pretty great for forty-three. A few lines around the eyes and mouth, but with a daily regime of tightening cream, gua sha, and moisturizer, her face could have remained smooth, supple, and youthful.

Reading about Dora's life, I find out she had no children and was never married, but raised her niece after her parents, Dora's brother and sister-in-law, were killed in a tragic car accident. Following her graduation from St. Killian University, Dora went to nursing school in the UK, then returned to the islands, where she took a job at a small clinic in St. Felipe. She remained in that position until a year ago when she left to become the Head Nurse at the Bee Well Medical Center.

Staring at Dora's photo on my computer screen, I wonder if she had low self-esteem. Or poor body image. Something convinced her that she didn't look good enough. Maybe she was dating someone who made her feel insecure about her looks. A shallow misogynist who pointed out an imaginary flaw on her face, which made her believe she had no choice but to resort to drastic measures to fit an unrealistic beauty standard.

Grabbing a pen and a notepad, I make a note to call Dora's niece for a comment about her aunt's passing. As I scan the obit for the niece's full name, I notice a comment beneath the post. *Adieu, my lovely friend. I will deeply miss you! Marlo Green.* Thinking it might be good to have another comment from someone else acquainted with Dora, I click the reply button.

*Good morning Ms. Green. My name is Sophie Carter. I'm a reporter at the Palmchat Gazette and would like to speak with you about Dora Butler. I am working on a story about her and would like more information about her life. Please contact me at the paper. I hope to hear from you. Thank you.*

Sighing, I check the clock on the computer. 8:07. A good a time as any to head to the breakroom for a cup of tea and—

Bing!

The sound comes from my computer, a familiar chime indicating the notification of an incoming message. Checking my inbox, I discover a reply from Marlo Green, Dora's friend. I open the message and read it.

*Ms. Carter, please call me at the following number. 555-0923. I really need to speak with you.*

Concerned by the seeming urgency, I pick up my desk phone and dial the number she gave me. Four rings later, and someone answers. "Hello?"

"Hi, this is Sophie Carter from the *Palmchat Gazette*—"

"Oh, Ms. Carter, I'm so glad you called," says a woman's hushed, hurried voice.

"Is this Marlo Green?" I ask, seeking confirmation.

"Yes, you sent me a message to contact you," says Marlo. "I was glad to hear from you. I was thinking about contacting the media, but I wasn't sure because the police won't listen to me, so … I figured the press might think I was crazy, too."

Confused, and trying to follow Marlo's quick cadence, I ask, "Ms. Green, why did you want to contact the media? What do you mean by the police won't listen to you?"

For a second, I'm worried that Marlo Green wants to vent about some trivial grievance, like people talking loudly on their phones in public or buses being a few minutes late, and hopes I'll give her free publicity.

But, then she says, "According to the article you wrote, the police think Dora accidentally poisoned herself with bee venom, but that's not what happened."

Grabbing my notebook and a pen, I say, "So, if that's not what happened, then … what happened to Dora?"

"Well, that's just it," says Marlo. "I don't know. But, I think the timing of her death is strange, considering …"

"Considering … what?"

"Dora was a nurse, very good at her job, but like a lot of health care workers, she suffered from burnout," says Marlo. "That can happen when there are so many sick patients and not enough time to give them all the attention they deserve."

"That's true," I agree, hoping she doesn't veer too far away from what she was considering.

"And Dora worked for a medical clinic in St. Felipe, on the most economically disadvantaged island in the Palmchat chain," Marlo continues. "Often, the hospital lacked the funds to obtain the equipment and medicine needed for its critical patients."

"So, Dora decided to change professions?" I ask.

"Somewhat," says Marlo. "She took the job at the medical spa because she could still use her nursing skills, or so she thought."

"What do you mean?"

"Turns out, she ended up as a glorified esthetician," says Marlo. "Most days, she was giving clients rejuvenating beeswax facial treatments."

"She wasn't using her nursing skills?"

"Not exactly," says Marlo. "But the medical spa wanted her to monitor the client's vital signs. You know, blood pressure, heart rate."

"Why did the clients have to have their vitals monitored while getting a facial?"

"Dora didn't know," says Marlo. "Or, rather she didn't tell me. But, she did mention that, after the beeswax facial, the clients seemed different."

"Different how?" I ask.

"Again, she didn't give me details," says Marlo. "But, she was very worried. She said there were odd things happening at the facility and she wanted to alert the authorities, but she didn't have all the evidence together."

"And she didn't mention what the odd things were?"

"I wish she had," says Marlo. "Then the police might have taken me seriously when I spoke to them about Dora's case."

"You told the police that Dora was trying to gather evidence about odd things happening at the medical center?" I ask, scribbling between the lines on my notepad.

Marlo says, "I told the cops that Dora was murdered."

"You think she was murdered?"

"And I told Detective François that an assistant beekeeper at the Bee Well Medical Center did it," says Marlo. "A woman named Ida. Dora told me she didn't trust Ida and was afraid of the woman."

"Why would Ida want to kill Dora?"

"Remember those odd things happening at the medical center?" asks Marlo. "Dora thought Ida had something to do with that shady business. I think Ida found out that Dora was on to her and killed Dora to keep her quiet ..."

# Chapter 9

Twenty minutes later, in the breakroom of the *Palmchat Gazette*, I'm sitting at a table with my coworkers Clark, and Candace, the office receptionist.

After the disturbing conversation with Marlo Green, I made notes in my green spiral tablet about what she told me, then thought about dabbling in a bit of speculation. However, I always do better at speculating when I'm drinking tea and eating donut holes, particularly honeysuckle and mint tea and fig glazed donut holes, but I've also speculated while having hibiscus tea and sugary pear donut holes, so there's that. Anyhoo, the point is, I decided to head to the breakroom.

Following greetings to Clark, who was drinking black coffee (don't ask me how) and Candace, sipping her specialty water, I brewed jasmine and blood orange tea to pair with chocolate glazed donut holes. Now, in the interest of full disclosure, and because I am a journalist with integrity, I am not certain that this combination will produce any decent speculative efforts, but anything is possible, right?

"So Marlo Green told the cops that an assistant beekeeper at the Bee Well Medical Center named Ida killed Dora," says Clark.

While making my tea, I filled Clark and Candace in on the worrisome conversation.

"Right," I say, recalling the conversation with Dora's good friend.

"Did Marlo say why she thinks Ida murdered Dora?" asks Clark.

"Marlo thinks Dora believed Ida was involved in some strange shenanigans going on at the medical center," I say. "Ida killed Dora so she wouldn't tell the cops."

"Strange shenanigans," muses Candace. "What did she mean by that?"

"Marlo didn't know because Dora didn't tell her," I say. "But she mentioned that Dora was trying to gather evidence to take to the police."

Tilting her head, Candace asks, "What if it wasn't Ida the assistant beekeeper? What if the owner of the medical center killed Dora because she was going to expose him?"

"Marlo was pretty adamant about Ida being involved in the shady business and killing Dora," I say, making a mental note to try and secure an interview with the medical center's founder. "But, that's just Marlo's opinion, which could be wrong. The founder of the center could be a suspect."

"That's what I would do," says Candace, taking another sip of water.

Clark frowns. "That's what you would do about what?"

"If I owned a business and I was engaging in shady shenanigans and I learned that one of my employees was going to expose me," says Candace, "I would get rid of that employee."

I glance at Clark, not shocked to find a shocked expression on his face, then ask, "What do you mean, you would get rid of the employee? Fire the employee?"

"I would do the same thing Dora's employer might have done to her," says Candace. "I'd kill the employee."

Gaping, I stare at Candace. "Are you serious?"

"It's not like I would have a choice," says Candace. "I wouldn't want to be exposed, ruined, and locked up for the rest of my life."

"But what if the police discover that you murdered your employee," says Clark. "You would still end up ruined and locked up for the rest of your life."

Standing, Candace says, "Trust me, Clark, I wouldn't get caught."

Seconds later, after Candace leaves the breakroom, whistling a jaunty tune as she power walks away, I look at Clark. "It might just be me, but I absolutely believe Candace would get away with murder."

Clark shakes his head. "It's not just you."

Ten minutes later, still pondering Candace's murderous admission, I'm back at my desk.

My thoughts shift to what the Bee Well Medical Center receptionist told me about Dora stealing bee hives to inject venom into her face to look younger. But is that true? Did Dora steal the bee hives? True, the spa reported the hives missing, but that doesn't mean Dora stole them. However, if she did, maybe she wasn't trying to look younger. Officer Cuetee pointed out that bee venom is used as a therapy for arthritis. Could Dora have had stiff joints? Could the pain have been so horrible and debilitating that she resorted to theft to get relief?

Leaning back in my chair, I drum my fingers against the desk.

Of course, Marlo's story warrants investigating. If Dora learned of something untoward, or even illegal, going on at the spa, and she planned to inform the police, could someone at the clinic have decided to silence her—for good?

The real question, naturally, is how do I find out?

Grabbing a pen, I scribble a list of people I'd like to talk to. First, is the spa owner. And, I'd like to chat with the receptionist again. And then I could talk to … who? Definitely Ida, the assistant beekeeper Marlo Green mentioned. Maybe other coworkers? Friends? But I have to find out who these people would be. Who would know?

Dora's niece comes to mind.

Having been raised by her aunt, the niece might be a good source, providing information about other people to interview. I access the public records database and type in her name. Butler, Samantha. I get twenty hits, but I'm able to narrow them down to four who live in St. Mateo.

On the second try, I reach Dora's niece.

After introducing myself, and explaining the story I'm doing on her aunt, I ask, "What do you think about how she died? I mean, considering that she was found covered in bees, but according to the medical examiner, she wasn't stung."

"I find it quite odd," says Samantha Butler. "And a little unbelievable. I wonder how competent the medical examiner is. My husband wonders if we should hire an outside independent forensic examiner."

"What do you think about the fact that high amounts of bee venom were in her blood?"

"I know what the medical spa thinks, but there is no way my aunt injected herself to look younger," says Samantha. "My aunt's skin was smoother and more supple than most twenty-year-olds. Most of the spa's clients believed she used the beeswax facials, but she didn't. My aunt's routine was simple. A gentle cleanser, moisturizer, and sunscreen. Good genetics helped, too."

"Do you have any thoughts on why there was so much venom in her blood?" I ask, jotting notes on my green Steno pad.

"I have no idea," says Samantha. "It makes no sense."

"Was she arthritic, maybe?"

"Arthritic? My aunt?" Samantha's voice rises with incredulity.

"Hardly. She ran every morning. Hiked. Swam. She was a beautiful, vivacious, active woman."

"What do you think could have happened to her?" I ask.

There's a pause, and then Samantha says, "I'm not sure …"

"So, you don't have any idea—"

"No, I mean … " Samantha sighs. "I'm not sure how to say this … I don't want to sound … "

"What is it?" I ask.

"It's just that," she starts, "before she died, my aunt told me that strange things were happening at the medical spa …"

A jolt of excitement travels through me. "What kind of strange things?"

"She never told me," says Samantha. "She said she couldn't go into details."

"Why not?"

Samantha says, "My aunt was afraid she would lose her job."

# Chapter 10

"Why was Dora afraid she would lose her job?" asks Callie, settling into the passenger seat of my car.

"Her niece didn't know," I say. "She thought maybe her aunt had signed an NDA, but she wasn't sure."

"An NDA?" Callie licks her paw. "Girl, what is that? Some kind of weird human tomfoolery that seems important but makes no sense."

Chuckling as I make the turn into the traffic on St. Mateo Way, the main boulevard dissecting downtown, I say, "Some people think so. However, an NDA is a Non-disclosure Agreement, and they are quite common.

It's been half an hour since my conversation with Dora Butler's niece, Samantha Butler. As soon as I hung up the phone, I made more notes on my green Steno pad, including a list of things to investigate next, then grabbed my purse and key, and left the building. Hurrying to my JEEP, I spotted the Calico in her customary place—the hood of my car. Following customary greetings, we jumped inside the vehicle, and I steered out of the parking lot.

"Non-disclosure Agreement," repeats Callie. "Meaning a

document humans sign so they can't spill the beans about something."

"Or so they won't let the cat out of the bag," I say, giggling.

The Calico gives me a look. "Girl, leave the cat idioms to me, okay?"

Rolling my eyes good-naturedly, I say, "Anyhoo … an NDA is a contract to keep information confidential."

"So, if Dora did sign an NDA, and then found out some shady stuff about the medical spa, she would lose her job for talking to the police," surmises Callie.

"Actually, no," I say, recalling my extensive research into NDAs, following the conversation with Samantha. "An NDA can't be used to hide illegal activity. Your boss can't make you sign an NDA forcing you to stay quiet if he breaks the law."

"So, Dora could have told the police," says Callie, licking her neck.

"Right," I confirm. "But Marlo said Dora was trying to gather evidence. So maybe she hadn't gone to the cops because she didn't have all her ducks in a row. Oops, sorry."

"For what?"

"You told me to leave the idioms to you."

"Girl, I said cat idioms," clarifies the Calico. "I don't care about waterfowl."

"Good to know," I say.

"But, wait," says Callie. "If Dora thought her employer was doing something illegal, then she could have told her niece about it, and she wouldn't have violated the NDA."

"True," I agree. "But, maybe Dora didn't know that. And, remember, we don't know if she signed an NDA. Maybe she didn't."

"Speaking of things not known," says the cat. "Where are we heading?"

"When I spoke to Dora's niece," I say, "she told me to visit Dora's neighbor, whose name I can't remember, but I did write it down."

"Girl, are you sure?" asks Callie. "You know how you are about not writing things down. That's how you ended up at the wrong place when you orchestrated that ill-fated sting to catch that dognapper."

"True," I agree, trying not to wince. Admittedly, I am not the best at setting up successful sting operations. "But, I did write the name down."

"Let's hope so," says Callie. "I don't want to end up at the wrong neighbor's house."

Twenty minutes later, I park along the curb in front of a small, well-maintained house the color of mint ice cream in the neighborhood of Tobacco Coast. I always find the name Tobacco Coast funny because the enclave of chattel homes is nowhere near the coast, but surrounded by lush rainforest. However, Tobacco Coast isn't exactly a misnomer because the area is close to an old, abandoned tobacco plantation.

"Is this neighbor expecting you?" asks the cat, rising on her hind legs, and balancing her front paws against the head rest as she tries to look past me toward the house.

"I don't think so," I say, removing my Steno pad from my purse and flipping to the page where I wrote the neighbor's name.

"What if she's not home?" asks Callie. "We would have come all this way for nothing."

"Think *pawsitively*," I say, giving her a wink.

The Calico gives me a look.

"Sorry," I say, giggling as I open the door. The cat leaps out, landing on the grass, then trots up the paved walkway to the porch. After locking the JEEP, I follow her.

At the door, I look down at Callie and say, "I should probably hold you."

"For what?" Callie challenges. "I'm not a kitten. I can walk."

"Well, Winifred East—that's the neighbor's name—might wonder why I showed up at her house with a cat," I explain.

The cat gives me a look. "And you don't think she'll question why you showed up at her house holding a cat in your arms?"

Biting my lower lip, I say, "You have a point."

"Girl, either way, you'd have to explain," says Callie. "And no matter what, it probably won't make sense. So, how about this—you talk to the neighbor, and I'll scope out the neighborhood."

"I don't know about that," I say, worried. "Tobacco Coast is close to the rainforest. Dangerous animals live in the jungle."

"Girl, I'm not scared of the jungle," says Callie. "When I was a kitten, I used to … "

"You used to … what?" I ask, curious.

The cat looks away. "Nothing, girl. You know me. I'll be fine. I'll catch up with you later and you can tell me what the neighbor said."

"Callie, I don't think—"

My protest is too late.

The Calico is already scampering down the steps of the porch, running across the street, and out of sight.

Sighing, I realize that Callie took off because she couldn't remember what she used to do as a kitten. The catnesia she suffers from often makes itself known during conversations when we're not discussing Callie's past, which remains a mystery to both of us.

And, usually, Callie avoids any further discussion and takes off. I'm not sure why. Maybe the memory loss is too painful and frustrating. Callie is fiercely independent and strong-willed. Perhaps the catnesia makes her feel weak, or as though she should be pitied.

I'd like to talk to her about the catnesia, but I know I can't force her.

She's a cat, after all. Meaning, she's not going to do anything she doesn't want to do.

Resigned, I face the door and ring the bell.

# Chapter 11

"The last time I saw Dora," says Winifred East, "she was arguing on her front porch with someone."

Following a quick sip of the tea Winifred offered me after she invited me to sit at the table in her dining room so we could chat, I ask, "Do you know who it was?"

Callie will be happy to know that not only was Winifred East home, but she was glad to see me because Samantha Butler had phoned her to let her know a reporter from the *Palmchat Gazette* might stop by.

"I have no idea who he was or his name," says Winifred, a petite West Indian woman who reminds me of an active grandmotherly type, wearing leggings, a fitted T-shirt, and running shoes. In fact, she'd just finished a three-mile jaunt with her senior running club, which Dora was part of, despite being only forty-three, the youngest of their group. "Honestly, I had never seen him before."

"You think he might have been a boyfriend?" I ask, then take another sip of tea, a delightful combination of raspberry and lemon, which I am sure would go fantastic with lemon-glazed or raspberry-glazed donut holes.

"Oh, goodness, I hope not," exclaims Winifred. "The way he was carrying on. I don't like to be a nosy neighbor, but he was mad as a wet goat about something. I couldn't tell what because it was raining that night, thundering something awful, but I could tell he was shouting. I was very worried. I wondered if I should go across the street to her house, but I didn't want to get into her business. And then things quieted down a bit. So, I went to the window again, and when I looked out, I saw them getting into a car. I checked the time. It was sometime after ten at night."

"And you don't know where they went?"

Shaking her head, her expression grim, Winifred says, "No idea. No place good, if you ask me. Not that late at night."

"Did you ask Dora about the argument?"

"I never got a chance to," says Winifred, expelling a heavy sigh. "Dora never came home. Next thing I heard was some folks found her dead on the beach. Had to have been that man, whoever he was, that done it, you ask me. That's what I told the detective who came to talk to me."

"Detective François."

Winifred nods. "The one whose *grandpere* caught the Fury."

Shuddering, I try not to dwell on any thoughts of the Fury—the heinous serial killer who stalked the Palmchat Islands more than forty years ago, but it's almost impossible. Just saying The Fury makes me think of the stories my grandparents and elderly great-aunts told me about the killer's sick, twisted reign of terror.

"I was a teenager back then," says Winifred, a trace of fear crossing her careworn features. "Scary times."

Anxious to get back to the subject, I ask, "What did Detective François say?"

"Not sure he took me seriously," admits Winifred. "Because of the rain. Was I sure they were arguing? Did the man look threatening or aggressive? Was I sure they weren't having a lover's spat? Well, I didn't think Dora was seeing anyone, but I couldn't be sure. Got the feeling he thought I was a gossipy, old busybody. Not sure if he investigated the car they drove off in, or not, but I gave him the license number."

Intrigued, I ask, "Do you still have it?"

Nodding, Winifred stands. "I wrote it in my address book. Let me get it."

As Winifred hurries out of the small dining area, I decide to engage in a bit of speculation about the man Dora argued with on her porch during a thunderstorm. Normally, I like peppermint tea when I'm speculating, but this lemon and raspberry will be fine, I'm sure.

I think this man, whoever he is, was probably the last person to see Dora alive. But that doesn't mean he killed her. However they were arguing, so he was upset with her. Still, that doesn't mean he killed her.

Maybe it was a lover's quarrel since Dora left with him. Would she have driven off into the night with a guy she feared might hurt her? Well, no, obviously not. However—

"Here it is," announces Winifred, returning to the dining room.

"Thanks," I say, placing the slip of paper in my cross body before taking the last sip of tea. "Anything else you can tell me about the man Dora argued with? Do you remember what he looked like?"

"Tall and thin," says Winifred. "That's all I can remember about him. Didn't see his face. Looked West Indian, though. Local Palmchatter, I reckon."

"Before I go," I say, standing. "I want to ask you if Dora ever mentioned anything about strange things going on at her job, the Bee Well Medical Center."

"No, she never told me anything strange was going on," says Winifred. "But she did tell me that she didn't trust one of her coworkers. A woman she thought was friendly but turned out to be her worst enemy."

"Did she tell you the coworker's name?" I ask, wondering if the coworker should be added to the suspect list. "Was it Ida?"

"Ida? I don't think so. The name doesn't sound familiar. Honestly, I don't remember her mentioning a name, but I wish she had," says Winifred, shaking her head. "I could have told the police about the coworker, now that I think about it. Dora said the coworker threatened her about something, I don't know what. Dora didn't want to get into it. But, the coworker told Dora to stay out of her way, or Dora would be sorry ..."

# Chapter 12

"Glad the neighbor gave you some good leads, sis," says Callie, walking across the breakfast bar, then leaping gracefully onto the table in the breakfast nook, where I'm enjoying a hot cup of orange and cinnamon tea with cinnamon-dusted donut holes—even though it's late afternoon.

"It was a very *pawsitive* experience," I say, unable to avoid risking Callie's wrath as I shove a donut hole into my mouth.

"Girl, what did I tell you?" demands the cat, her back arched as she hisses at me.

"Sorry, couldn't resist."

"You humans never can," comments the cat, settling herself into a "loaf" position. "But, it's all puns and games until you get your eyes scratched right out of your head!"

Stifling a laugh at Callie's favorite threat, I take another sip of tea and then put the mug down. "Okay, ready for the not-so-good news?"

"How is there bad news?" asks the Calico. "The neighbor gave you a suspect to investigate. Some mysterious guy who argued with Dora and drove away with her in his car."

"His car," I say, recalling the research I did yesterday after I returned to the *Palmchat Gazette* offices, following the meeting with Winifred East. "The bad news is I wasn't able to find out the mystery guy's name because the license plate was registered to the Bee Well Medical Center."

"And how is that bad news?" asks Callie, rising to all fours.

"I was hoping to find his name," I lament. "But I learned he drove Dora away in a company car."

"Well, at least you know this," says the cat. "The guy she argued with must have worked at the medical center, as well."

"You're right," I say, feeling foolish. "He's obviously a coworker, too."

"You could easily find out," says Callie, licking her paw.

Nodding, I pop another donut hole in my mouth, chew thoughtfully, then swallow. "You know, if what Marlo Green and Dora's niece Samantha said is true about Dora thinking something strange was going on at the medical spa and she was compiling evidence to take to the police then ..."

"Then?" prompts the cat.

"Then maybe her coworker found out," I say. "Winifred East says Dora and the guy were arguing. About what? Maybe Dora confronted him about the strange happenings at the clinic. And maybe he ..."

"Got rid of Dora so she couldn't go to the police?" asks Callie, licking her hind leg.

"It's definitely *pawssible*," I say, once again, unable to resist the cat pun.

"Girl, do you like being able to see?" Callie hisses.

I suppress my giggles. "Sorry. Sorry. Yes, it's possible the coworker Dora argued with could have killed her. If he works at the medical center, then he has access to bee venom."

"And to dead bees," says Callie.

"If the coworker killed Dora, how do I prove it?" I ask, drumming my fingers against the table.

"Girl, the way I see it," says Callie. "You have to find out more about the strange happenings at the spa. If you come up with a motive for the coworker, then maybe the detective will take you seriously and take a more critical look at the case."

"You're right," I tell the cat. "I need to figure out what was going on. What evidence was Dora collecting? And who is the mystery guy she argued with?"

"Don't forget about the other coworker," says the cat, licking her neck. "The assistant beekeeper."

"That's right," I say. "A woman Dora worked with who threatened her. Told Dora she would be sorry if she didn't leave her alone, something like that. But was that female coworker Ida, the assistant beekeeper?"

"Girl, the way I see it is there's the male coworker Dora argued with in the rain the night before she was found dead," says the cat, licking her paw. "And then there's Ida the assistant beekeeper, who may or may not be the female coworker who threatened Dora. Suffice it to say, Dora was trying to get evidence against one of her coworkers."

Nodding, I say, "I've got to figure out which one. That's the coworker who might have killed her …"

# Chapter 13

"I'm on a break and wanted to call you because I have some information about the Dora Butler case," says Officer Cuetee, after we engage in morning greetings and small talk, which is largely about tea and donut hole combinations.

I was actually on my way to the break room for a cup of jasmine tea to start my day when my desk phone rang. Hearing Officer Cuetee's voice gave me a thrill, and not only because he has a nice, raspy, deep voice but also because I've been waiting to hear from him.

Three days ago, I met with him for a quick lunch at R.S. Tea, a lovely tea café near the library that has beachy boho vibes, and asked for help with the Dora Butler murder case.

"And so I think one of her coworkers might have killed her," I concluded after telling Officer Cuetee about my conversations with Marlo Green, Samantha Butler, and Winifred East. "I think the female coworker is an assistant beekeeper named Ida, but I'm not sure about her last name. The male coworker argued with Dora, then they left her house in a company car. I need help figuring out who he is and what happened the night he argued with Dora."

Officer Cuetee agreed that both coworkers seemed suspicious and warranted more investigation. He promised to let me know if he discovered any additional details.

Grabbing a pen, I flip to a blank page in my Steno pad, then ask, "Did you find out any details about François's investigation of the assistant beekeeper, Ida, as a murder suspect? Or the name of Dora's male coworker?"

"François is keeping his cards close to the vest about Ida," says Officer Cuetee. "However, I was able to find out where Dora and the mystery male coworker went when they left in the company car."

"How?" I ask, absolutely impressed.

"CCTV," says Officer Cuetee. "There are a few traffic cameras on the main road out of Tobacco Coast. I picked up the car on one of those cameras and was able to track it to the Bee Well Day Spa."

"There's a Bee Well Day Spa?" I ask, trying to remember if I saw a second location on the website.

"Apparently," says Officer Cuetee. "Dora and the mystery coworker went inside the building. About an hour later, the coworker exited the day spa—alone."

"Where was Dora?"

"That's the weird thing," says Officer Cuetee. "Dora didn't leave the building. But, the mystery coworker drove to the ferry, where he parked the car in the lot, and then waited for the first boat, which arrived at five in the morning. I'm not sure where he went, though. I checked the manifest for the five-a.m. ferry and there were twenty-eight people who boarded. Most paid cash. Nine people paid with a credit card and those nine were tourists."

"Which means he probably paid cash so he could have sailed to any island in the Palmchat chain," I say.

"Right," says Officer Cuetee. "Good thing is, I spoke with Detective François. He's going to have a conversation with the employees at the day spa."

"Did the mystery coworker return to get his car?"

"He did," says Officer Cuetee. "He came back on the six-p.m. ferry. He got in the company car and drove back to the day spa. But, he didn't go inside. Instead, he crossed the street, then headed down a side street and out of sight of the cameras. I tried to find him on some other major cross streets, but no luck."

After my conversation with Officer Cuetee, I jot down notes about my thoughts.

First of all, why did Dora and the mystery coworker go to the day spa after ten at night? Obviously, the spa wasn't open. What happened in the day spa? Why didn't Dora leave the day spa with the mystery coworker? Was it because she couldn't? Because her coworker had killed her? If so, how did he remove her body from the day spa without being seen on the CCTV cameras?

Sighing, I tap my pen against the pad.

The day after Dora argued with her coworker, her body was found on the beach, covered in dead bees. How did that happen? Did the coworker kill Dora, then somehow, transport her dead body out of the day spa and leave it on the beach, covered in dead bees?

Plausible, I'm sure.

But provable?

I don't really know …

# Chapter 14

"Looks like there're two main suspects," says Clark.

At one in the afternoon, Clark, Candace, and I are taking a break, which Marty would probably think is not well-deserved, before our three o'clock staff meeting, where Marty will probably chew us out over trivial things. Per usual, I'm having tea—lime, and echinacea—Clark has black coffee, and Candace sips alkaline water.

Nodding, I agree. "The mystery coworkers. Whoever they are ..."

"The female coworker might be Ida," says Clark.

"Yeah, but I don't know her last name so I don't really know who she is, either."

"Well, if you knew who they were, they wouldn't be a mystery," says Candace.

"No, of course they wouldn't," I say, remembering how odd and literal Candace can be at times. "I'm just at a loss about how to figure out who they are."

"Is there an employee page on the website?" asks Clark. "You know, like, 'Meet our Team'?"

I shake my head. "There's only a photo of Dr. Napier, and he's a small, fat man. The very opposite of tall and thin, which was how Winifred East, Dora's neighbor, described the mystery coworker."

"You've got to go to the day spa," says Clark. "That's your best bet at finding out."

"That's what I'm thinking," I say, taking another sip of tea.

"That's your problem," says Candace.

"What's my problem?" I ask, frowning at Candace.

"Thinking," says Candace. "You're always thinking too much. Or not thinking enough."

Confused, I say, "I don't understand."

"Another problem of yours," says Candace, finishing her water. "Understanding. Sometimes you do. Sometimes you don't."

"Doesn't everybody?" asks Clark, frowning. "I mean, sometimes you understand something and sometimes you don't."

"Right," agrees Candace. "But you should be more consistent about your understanding, or lack thereof."

"I'm not following," I say, wondering, for the millionth time, why I even bother trying to talk to Candace.

"Another problem," announces Candace. "You're unwillingness to follow."

"I'm not unwilling to follow," I tell her. "I just don't follow what you're saying."

Shaking her head, giving me a look of pity, Candace says, "Sophie, when you say you don't do something, it means you're not willing to do the thing that you claim you don't do."

I tilt my head and stare at Candace, as if, somehow, that will help me understand her. "What?"

"Right, right," says Clark. "We get it now."

"I had no doubt that you would," says Candace. "I've got to get back to work. But, before I do, I meant to tell you, Sophie, that a friend of mine went to the Bee Well Medical Center."

"Really?" I ask, interested, wishing Candace had started with this topic of conversation.

"She got the beeswax facial and started acting differently."

"How?"

"She became very forgetful," says Candace. "For the first few weeks after she came home, she couldn't remember what happened at the medical center."

I glance at Clark, whose curious confusion mirrors mine. "That's strange."

"You want to know what was really strange?" asks Candace. "She didn't even look younger. So, for the life of me, I don't know why she donated to the medical center's charity, Save the Bees."

# Chapter 15

"Friends?" says Harriet Post. "Who told you Candace and I are friends?"

Sitting at my desk in my cubicle, I stare at the phone, which I have on speaker mode, hoping I can get information from Candace's friend—who may or may not be her friend—about her experience at the Bee Well Medical Center. Specifically, I want to ask her about the tall, thin man, and I'm curious to know if she might be able to tell me more about him.

"Oh, well, um, actually …" I clear my throat. "Candace told me that—"

"She would," says Harriet. "But we're not friends. Not anymore."

"Oh, I'm sorry to hear that," I say.

"Why would you be sorry that Candace and I aren't friends anymore?" asks Harriet. "I'm not."

"Oh, well, um, I just—"

"How did you get my number?" barks Harriet.

Worried, I say, "Candace gave it to me."

"Why would she do that?"

"Because she thought you might have some information about the Bee Well Medical Center."

"Why would she think that?"

"Um, because you went there to get a beeswax serum facial."

"How does Candace know that?"

"You must have told her."

"When?"

"Um ..." I trail off, remembering what Candace said about her friend's spotty memory. "I'm not sure. However, I was wondering if you could tell me more about your experience there."

Harriet says, "I don't know. I don't remember much about that place. Except for the smell of honey in my room all the time. Got on my nerves."

"Well, I mean, I suppose it's not surprising for the center to smell like honey," I say. "After all, they use bee products."

"But, the crazy thing was that I could only smell the honey in my room," says Harriet. "At first, I didn't understand why, but then I saw ..."

"You saw?"

"You know, I don't remember," says Harriet. "Probably wasn't important."

I'm inclined to disagree, but I ask, "Mrs. Post, do you recall any of the staff at the medical center? Do you remember any interactions with a tall, thin man?"

"Not exactly," she says. "Which doesn't mean that I didn't talk to him, though. Mainly, I remember this rude housekeeper. She kept cleaning my room, even when I told her not to. I didn't trust her. I think she was up to something."

"Up to what?"

"I don't remember," says Harriet.

"Ms. Post, I hope you don't find this question offensive," I start.

"But, before you went to the medical center, did you have memory problems? I only ask because Candace says your memory suffered after you returned from the center."

Harriet says, "Candace isn't the only one who says that. My husband and kids think the same thing. They're convinced one of the beeswax treatments caused memory impairment."

"Do you think that?" I ask, scribbling notes on my green Steno pad.

"I don't know what to think," Harriet says. "I've seen several doctors and none of them have found anything wrong, so ..."

"Interesting," I murmur, making more notes in my Steno pad.

"My kids think I got ripped off," says Mrs. Post.

"Because the serum didn't work?" I ask, recalling what Candace said about Harriet not looking any younger after visiting the medical center.

"Because I donated a bunch of money to the Save the Bees charity that the Bee Well Medical Center founded," says Harriet. "A hundred thousand dollars, or so they say."

"Or so they say?"

"I don't remember giving the donation," says Harriet. "But my signature was on the canceled check, and I had a receipt from the charity, thanking me for my generosity."

"Wow," I say, shocked, though I'm not surprised Mrs. Post has money, considering how much the Bee Well Medical Center costs. "That was very generous of you."

"Or very stupid of me," snorts Harriet. "Like my kids told me, which bees are being saved? And why do they need to be saved? Are bees an endangered species?"

"Actually," I say, "I'm not quite sure."

"But, it's not like I can ask for the money back," says Harriet. "And what's a hundred thousand dollars, anyway?"

"Okay, well," I say, deciding to wrap up the call, figuring that Mrs.

Post probably won't remember the answers to any other questions I might have. "I hope you have a great rest of the day and thank you for speaking with me."

"No problem, thank you," she says. "Oh, before you go … what was your name again? And why did you call me?"

# Chapter 16

"Hey, girl, hey!" Callie calls to me from her normal spot, the hood of my red JEEP.

Waving, I hurry across the *Palmchat Gazette* parking lot, shielding my eyes from the bright, early afternoon sunshine.

"Where have you been?" I ask Callie when I reach my vehicle.

"Girl, you know me," says Callie, licking her paw. "I've been around. Here and there. You headed out to cover a story?"

Shaking my head, I say, "Going to lunch. But speaking of covering stories, I have some new information about the Dora Butler murder."

"What's tea, sis?" asks Callie. "Do you know who killed her?"

"Not yet," I say. "But I have two suspects. I'll tell you about them on the way to the Loco Cabrito shack."

Minutes later, as I turn the JEEP into the traffic, I say, "So, you know about the two mystery coworkers …"

"Have you identified either one of them?" asks Callie, lying on the passenger seat.

"Unfortunately, no," I say. "But, Officer Cuetee used CCTV footage to find out that the male coworker who argued with Dora drove her to the Bee Well Day Spa."

"There's a day spa, too?"

"Apparently," I say, using my indicator before executing a lane change. "Anyway, Dora and the male coworker went into the day spa, but only the male coworker came out. There's no CCTV video of Dora leaving the day spa."

"Because she didn't," says the cat. "Because her coworker killed her."

"That's what I'm thinking," I say.

"So what are you doing to prove it?"

"Well, I'm trying to identify the coworkers," I say, maneuvering around the traffic circle. "I thought I had a lead from one of Candace's friends—who, it turns out, isn't really her friend. Don't ask."

"Girl, I wasn't going to," says the Calico. "I know better than to try to understand anything about that dingbat coworker of yours."

Giggling, I say, "Well, she has a friend who went to the medical center. So, I was hoping she could identify the tall, thin coworker, but she didn't remember him. In fact, she didn't remember much of anything about her time at the medical center. Candace had told me she suffered memory loss after she came back, and I think it's true."

"She has catnesia?" asks Callie.

I turn into the small parking lot of Loca Cabrito shack, then join the cars lined up for the drive-thru. "She can't have catnesia because she's not a cat."

"Girl, you know what I mean," hisses the cat.

"I don't think she has amnesia," I say. "She told me she's seen several doctors about the memory loss, but they can't find anything wrong. And yet, she doesn't even remember donating a hundred thousand dollars to the medical center's charity, Save the Bees. And a hundred thousand dollars is a lot of money."

"Girl, maybe to you but maybe not to her."

"Still," I say. "I'm sure she would have remembered. It seems she started losing her memory after she came back from the Bee Well Medical Center."

"You think she slipped, fell, and hit her head at the medical center?" asks Callie.

Considering Callie's suggestion, I say, "I suppose she might have suffered some sort of head trauma. But, wouldn't a doctor have been able to determine that?"

"Girl, forget about what a doctor can determine," advises Callie. "What are you going to do? How are you going to prove your theory about who killed Dora Butler?"

An hour later, sitting in my cubicle, stuffed from my lunch—jerk goat tacos—I'm still thinking about that challenge the feisty feline gave me. How am I going to prove that Dora Butler was killed by her coworker? Well, first I've got to find out the names of her coworkers, especially the guy she argued with. Which means, I need to take a trip to the day spa.

But, before I do, I'm going to research the Save the Bees charity. I figure I can use the charity as an excuse when I show up at the day spa. My plan is to pretend I want to donate, but I need more information about the charity. I need to find something on the charity's website to ask about.

Turning to my computer, I type 'save the bees charity' into the search engine and wait.

But nothing comes up.

Well, something comes up, but nothing that has anything to do with the Bee Well Medical Center's effort to save bees in St. Mateo. Biting my lower lip, I try a few more search combinations, including *save the bees st. mateo* and *bee well save the bees* and *bee well charity*.

But I don't get any results linking me to the charity Harriet Post donated to. Hmmm. Maybe the charity isn't called Save the Bees. Maybe that's the unofficial name. Maybe—

"Goofing off on the internet again?"

Rolling my eyes, I swivel around in my chair and face Clark. "Ha. Ha. If you must know, I am doing some research for the Dora Butler murder case."

Giving me a doubtful smirk, Clark asks, "What kind of research?"

I tell Clark about my conversation with Candace's friend who's not really her friend, including her memory loss and the large charitable donation she made to the medical center.

"But, I can't seem to find a website for the charity," I say, turning back to my computer. "I was hoping to find out more about it, then head to the Bee Well Day Spa and pretend that I wanted to donate."

"Maybe there is no website," suggests Clark.

"Don't you think the medical center would want the public to know about their efforts to save bees?"

"Maybe they don't want the public attention," reasons Clark. "Or the scrutiny. You know how judgy people can be about charities. There's always someone who thinks you're donating too much or not donating enough."

Nodding, I say, "Or thinking you should be donating to a better cause."

"That too," says Clark. "But, since you have to go to the day spa, you can ask about the charity."

"That was going to be my excuse for going anyway," I say.

"What are you going to say when they ask you how much you plan to donate?" Clark asks.

Scoffing, I say, "Definitely not a hundred thousand."

# Chapter 17

The Bee Well Day Spa is a large bungalow, painted a sunny yellow with white trim, located on the outskirts of Guavatown.

I arrive at ten a.m. in the morning, full of nervous anticipation and a smidge of doubt—because, let's face it, I'm not the world's best investigative reporter yet. Nevertheless, I have given myself an audacious, daunting goal, which is to find out the identity of Dora Butler's tall, thin coworker, the man she argued with in the rain on the night before she was found dead the next day.

Essentially, I am looking for a cold-blooded killer.

Now, of course, I don't know for certain if the tall, thin coworker killed Dora, but that's my theory, and until there is evidence to the contrary, I plan to stick with it and try to prove it. I don't think I'm off base, as I might have been in the past, because, based on what Officer Cuetee told me, the tall, thin coworker drove Dora to the Bee Well Day Spa, and then the two went inside. But only the tall, thin coworker came out. The next time anyone saw Dora was when her lifeless body, covered in dead bees, was discovered on the beach.

I park my JEEP in the lot behind the bungalow, which is empty except for a small hatchback, which I'm assuming belongs to an employee. I'm not sure if I'm the only patron, considering that others might have been dropped off, maybe by their chauffeurs—after all, the Bee Well Day Spa is pretty pricey.

Cutting the ignition, I check my reflection in my rearview mirror.

For this investigation, I've decided to portray myself as a spoiled island heiress.

Exiting the JEEP, I stride to the front door, making sure to walk with an air of confidence, like a West Indian "it girl." At the door, I take a quick breath and then walk inside. The air is cool and refreshing, with a faint scent of ... honey. Which isn't surprising. The spacious lobby is warm and inviting, with bamboo furniture, natural fiber rugs, potted palm trees, and walls the shade of whipped honey.

Behind the reception counter sits a young woman with red hair slicked back in a bun. She appears to be wearing crisp, wrinkle-free scrubs the color of – not surprisingly, honey. As I approach her, she gives me a pleasant smile, which highlights the smattering of freckles across her nose.

"Good morning," I say, adopting the tone of cultured Caribbean royalty, which is a soft-spoken lilt with a hint of haughtiness and elegance. "How are you today?"

"Good morning, I'm well," says the receptionist, whose gold-plated oval nameplate says Opal. "Thank you for asking and how may I help you? Do you have an appointment today?"

"No, actually, I am curious about something," I say. "My name is Sophia Cartier and I was hoping to speak with one of the Bee Well staff associates, however, I am embarrassed to admit that I have forgotten his name. If I described him, could you remind me? When I speak with him, I don't want to be uncouth."

"I'll certainly try," says Opal. "What does he look like?"

"Well, he is, um ... " I clear my throat, realizing that my description of Dora's male coworker is woefully inadequate. But maybe Opal will know him. "He's rather tall ..."

Opal frowns. "Rather tall?"

Nodding, fighting disappointment, I say, "And quite thin …"

"Rather tall and quite thin," repeats Opal, looking doubtful. "Hmmm … doesn't sound familiar to me."

"Oh … well, that's unfortunate," I say, wondering what else I could say to jog her memory.

"But, maybe I just don't know him," Opal says. "If he works at the medical center on Bee Island, then it's likely I've never met him."

"Bee Island …" I murmur, trying to recall if I've heard of it.

"That's where the Bee Well Medical Center is located," says Opal. "That's not the official name. I'm not sure there is one, but we call it Bee Island."

Nodding, I say," So, employees who work at the day spa and those who work at the medical center never work together?"

Shaking her head, Opal says, "Right. As a matter of fact, I don't have any coworkers here."

"You don't?"

"I work alone," says Opal.

Confused, I ask, "So, when you do the treatments, who works the reception desk? If you don't mind me asking. I just—"

"Oh no, it's fine," says Opal, smiling. "No one gets treatments here, even though it's called the Bee Well Day Spa. This is where clients come to pay for treatments they plan to get on the island and to support the charity … "

"The charity?" I ask, even though I know what she's talking about.

"Save the Bees," says Opal.

"I've never heard of it," I say.

"You wouldn't have unless you visited the Bee Well Medical Center," says Opal. "Are you interested in visiting the center?"

"Yes, I am," I say. "That's why I was hoping to speak with the … tall, thin gentleman I met last week … but—"

A soft chime interrupts me as I hear a door open.

Looking past me, Opal smiles, and I glance over my shoulder.

An older woman, fifty-or-sixty-something years old, ambles into the day spa. Dressed like a Caribbean country club socialite, in a bright pastel dress complimented by tasteful, but expensive jewelry, she says, "Opal, dear, so lovely to see you!"

"Hello Mrs. DuFault, it's lovely to see you, as well," says Opal. "I'll be with you in a moment."

"Oh, take your time, dear," says Mrs. DuFault, taking a seat in one of the bamboo chairs in the lobby nook. "I'm just dropping off my monthly donation."

Monthly donation, I think, my curiosity piqued.

Opal says, "Would you mind if I take care of Mrs. DuFault? It won't take long. Then we can discuss setting up an appointment at the medical center for you."

"Oh, actually, I'll have to ask my husband about the medical center," I say, a spur-of-the-moment plan forming in my mind. "I'll get out of your hair for now but thank you for speaking with me."

# Chapter 18

"Excuse me, Mrs. DuFault ... "

The Caribbean socialite turns, then frowns as I approach her car, a large silver Mercedes. Hopefully, I look like a West Indian debutante and not a crazy woman. Smiling, I try to appear delicate and elegant, but I'm well aware this woman doesn't know me from a goat in a boat. Still, I've got to try to execute the plan that came to me, which is to find out more about the Save the Bees charity. I figured I might get more out of Mrs. DuFault than I would from Opal.

"Yes ..." says Mrs. DuFault, giving me a wary glance. "Do I know you?"

"Oh, I saw you inside the day spa," I say. "And wanted to speak with you."

"Oh, yes," she says, still a bit wary, but appearing to recall me. "What can I do for you?"

"Well, my name is Sophia Cartier," I say, using the spoiled West Indian heiress name I made up. "And I wanted to ask you about the charity."

"What charity?"

"Save the Bees."

"Oh, yes … Save the Bees."

"I'm thinking of donating to it … can you tell me more about it?"

Mrs. DuFault looks confused. "More about what?"

"The Save the Bees charity?"

"What more do you want to know about it?"

"Well, can you tell me the purpose of the charity?" I ask. "I assume to save bees, but—"

"Oh, dear, I have no idea," says Mrs. DuFault, giving me a breezy, dismissive wave. "I just support it. My donation is ten thousand dollars a month."

"Ten thousand dollars a month," I repeat, mouth agape, until I remember that, as a West Indian heiress, ten thousand a month shouldn't shock me. "How kind and generous of you!"

"To whom much is given, much is required, of course," says Mrs. DuFault. "I must do my part as one of the more fortunate."

"I agree," I say.

"That's why, when I get the call, I donate," says Mrs. DuFault.

"What call?" I ask.

Shrugging, Mrs. DuFault says, "Well, I get a phone call, and then … "

"And then … what happens?"

Frowning, she says, "Well, I answer but no one says anything."

"They don't?"

"There's just … buzzing."

"Buzzing?"

Nodding, Mrs. DuFault says, "Like a bee … like thousands of bees … and that's how I know it's time to donate."

Interesting, I think, then ask, "And when did you decide to start donating to the charity?"

"After I went to the spa last year," she says. "Although, I'm not sure the treatments worked. I don't recall much from my experience there … "

"You don't?" I ask, intrigued by how similar her story is to Candace's not-exactly-friend, Mrs. Post.

"Except, the honey spray," says Mrs. DuFault, nose wrinkling. "The housekeeper was always spraying it in my room before I went to bed, even when I told her not to. I don't like the smell of honey."

"Some do and some don't," I say, my mind spinning with questions about the Bee Well Medical Center, the Save the Bees charity, and the odd loss of memory suffered by Mrs. Post and Mrs. DuFault. I have an urge to speculate, but I speculate best with peppermint tea, so I'd rather wait, as I don't want to waste time jumping to the wrong conclusions.

"Do you plan to visit the Bee Well Medical Center?" asks Mrs. DuFault, eyeing me with what seems like skepticism.

"I was thinking about it," I answer.

Mrs. DuFault looks aghast. "But, you're so young! Your skin is flawless."

"Well, you can never start too early, right?" I say, smiling. "After all, we have to deal with this harsh Caribbean sun."

"That's true," she says. "Well, if you need a referral, I'll be happy to give you one. Tell them Felice DuFault sent you!

"So, let me get this straight, sis," says Callie, sitting on the hood of my red JEEP. "Clients go to the medical center, get treatments, don't remember what happened at the medical center but end up giving large donations to the Save the Bees charity?"

"That's right," I say, leaning against the driver's door. "So far, I have evidence of two people visiting the medical center, suffering memory loss, and giving donations to a mysterious bee-saving charity."

Following my visit to the Bee Well Day Spa this morning, I returned to the *Palmchat Gazette*, where I had every intention of making a cup of peppermint tea so I could properly and efficiently speculate about the medical center, the memory loss, and the donations to the Save the Bees charity.

However, Marty had other ideas.

Those ideas being sending me out to cover a story.

After gathering the detailed details, I grabbed lunch, then returned to the newspaper's offices, and wrote my first draft. Surprisingly, Marty said it was "better than usual" and only had a few revisions, however, he made it clear that I'm still not off the hook. My investigative skills are improving, but I can't slack off. He remains determined to "ship me out" if I don't "shape up."

By the time my story was published on the paper's website, it was time to call it a day, which I did, gathering my things and heading out to my car, where I saw the Calico.

Callie says, "Sounds like the Bee Well Medical Center is running some kind of scam."

"I agree," I say. "The medical center is, somehow, causing memory loss while at the same time receiving donations to their bee saving charity."

Callie says, "Maybe they don't want people to remember donating, so they won't ask for their money back."

"You might be right," I say. "What if Mrs. Post and Mrs. DuFault didn't want to donate or declined to donate? But, somehow, the medical center convinced them to donate. Maybe they forced them to donate? Or tricked them into signing something? And so, they don't want them to remember being forced or tricked, so they gave them something that caused the memory loss."

"But what could have caused the memory loss?" asks the Calico, licking her paw.

"I'm not sure," I say. "But you remember I told you that Dora's friend, Marlo, and her niece, Samantha, said Dora was concerned about something odd going on at the medical center? Maybe Dora noticed that clients were having memory problems after visiting the medical center."

"Girl, you might be on to something."

I look at the cat. "Dora might have been gathering evidence to prove that the medical spa was causing memory loss to scam money from the clients."

"Maybe that's why her coworker killed her," suggests Callie.

"You could be right," I say. "Question is, how do I prove it?"

# Chapter 19

"Where are we headed, sis?" asks Callie, sitting in the passenger seat of my JEEP.

Two days have passed since my visit to the Bee Well Day Spa. Since then, I've been busy with other stories that Marty has assigned to me, but unfortunately, I haven't had time to think much about how to prove my theory that Dora Butler was killed by her co-worker because she discovered that the medical center is running a scam.

Nevertheless, this morning, I got an email from Dora's niece Samantha, asking if I'd heard anything from the police about her aunt's case. She's been trying to convince the police to investigate her aunt's death as a homicide, and not an accidental overdose. I was sorry to tell her I didn't have any information, but I shared my theory about Dora's suspicious co-worker.

"I think maybe your aunt was gathering information to expose the medical center," I said. "I'm just trying to figure out how to prove it."

"Maybe Aunt Dora was keeping this evidence at her house," Samantha said.

"That's possible," I said. "Maybe you could go through some of her belongings and see if you find anything."

"I wish I could," said Samantha. "Unfortunately, I had to head out of the country for work and I won't be back for another few weeks."

"That's too bad," I lamented.

"But maybe you could take a look around," suggested Samantha. "My aunt always kept a spare key beneath the hibiscus plant on her porch. So, you could get into the house."

"And you would be okay with that?"

"If it means finding some sort of proof that my aunt was murdered, absolutely," said Samantha.

As I steer the JEEP into the midmorning traffic on St. Mateo Way, I glance at the cat. "We're going to Dora Butler's house to look for clues."

"How are we going to get in?" asks the cat.

I tell her, and then say, "I'm not sure we'll find anything, but I figure we have to try."

Twenty minutes later, the cat and I are standing on the porch of Dora Butler's small chattel house in Tobacco Coast.

"Girl, what are you waiting for?" asks Callie, staring up at me. "You got the key from the hibiscus bush. Let's go inside."

"Okay, okay," I tell the Calico as I insert the key into the lock.

Opening the door, I take a quick breath before entering but Callie hurries inside. "Wait, wait ..."

Crossing the threshold into Dora's house, I glance around. The place is small but neat and simply furnished with pieces that take into consideration the lack of space. A beige sofa against the wall is anchored by square wooden end tables. Across from the couch, a television sits on a matching wood console. Beyond the living area is an open L-shaped kitchen with a bistro table and four chairs.

Glancing back at me, Callie asks, "Wait for what? Girl, I got other things to do. Let's search this place, find what clues we can, and scram."

"But that's just it," I say, closing the door behind me.

"What's just it?"

"I'm not quite sure what I'm looking for," I admit.

"Proof that Dora's coworker killed her," says Callie, leaping onto the couch. "Evidence of shenanigans going on at the medical center."

"I know that," I say. "But where would she have kept this proof?"

"Where do you humans usually keep things hidden?" asks the cat.

"Places where those things can't be found," I say, looking around the living area. "I need to check the cabinets in the kitchen. And the drawers, too."

"And I'll shimmy under the couch and behind the end tables," says Callie.

With our plan in place, we start our search.

Fifteen minutes later, we convene at the bistro table, both of us empty-handed.

"All I found were pots and pans and knives and spoons and forks," I grumble.

Licking her hind leg, Callie says, "Girl, I got dust bunnies bigger than the hairballs I cough up."

Tempering my disappointment, I say, "Why do I have a feeling the bathroom and bedroom will be no different?"

"We still have to look, sis," says Callie. "I'll check out the bedroom. You take the bathroom."

I give the cat a look. "And how are you going to open the bureau drawers?"

"Girl, please," says Callie, scampering away. "Cats can open drawers, doors … we can get into anything."

"Why am I not surprised?" I say, laughing as I head down a short hall and turn into the bathroom. There's a shower, toilet, and pedestal sink below a round mirror. No cabinets to search, but on top of the toilet tank lid, there's a wicker basket slightly bigger than a breadbox. Opening it, I glance inside. Lots of beauty products. Lipsticks, blushes, eyeshadow palettes, cleansers, and—

"Girl, you're not a cat, stop playing in that box ..."

Pivoting toward the door, I stare at the Calico. "What?"

"I think I found something in the bedroom!" Callie announces then dashes away.

"Wait! What?" I ask, rushing after the cat. "

Jumping onto the bed table, Callie says, "It's under the bed."

"What is it?" I ask, taking a knee next to the bed, then lowering down to peek beneath it.

"Some kind of book."

Spotting what looks like a spiral journal, I reach under the mattress, grab it, and pull it out. Sitting on my knees, I open the journal and flip through the pages.

"What is it?" asks Callie.

Glancing at the cat, I say, "I think this is a diary ..."

# Chapter 20

"A diary?" Callie leaps onto the bed. "What does it say?"

Standing, I dust myself off, then sit next to the cat. "I don't know. I haven't read it."

"Girl, what are you waiting for?" asked the Calico. "Stop staring at the diary and open it."

Hesitating, I say, "You think I should? A diary is personal. These are Dora Butler's private thoughts."

"So?" demands Callie.

"So … maybe she wanted the contents of this journal to remain private," I say.

The cat gives me a look. "Girl, Dora's niece told you to look for clues. That diary could be a clue!"

"I suppose you're right," I say.

"Girl, I know I'm right," says the Calico. "How many times do I have to tell you? Cats know things."

"Okay, okay," I say, placing the journal on my lap, and then opening it.

"What does it say?" demands Callie, patting my hand with her paw.

"Give me a sec," I tell her, flipping the blank pages. "There's nothing on these first pages but I'm sure I saw something toward the middle ..."

"That's strange," says the cat. "Don't you humans usually start writing on the first page?"

"Yes, we do," I say, still flipping pages. "But ... oh, wait a second. I think I found something ..."

"Don't keep me in suspense, sis," says Callie. "You know cats are curious."

"Okay, okay ..." I say, staring at the small, neat writing on the page. "It's dated ... four months ago. And it says, *'don't trust worker bee #4'* ... hmmm ..."

"Is that it?" asks the cat.

"That's the only thing written on this page," I say. "Which is kind of weird because normally people write more than one sentence on a journal page."

"What do you think she meant?" Callie asks.

"Not sure," I admit. "Dora could have meant that she doesn't trust worker bee #4. Or, she could have meant that worker bee #4 is not to be trusted."

"Girl, isn't that the same thing?"

"Possibly," I concede. "No matter what, there were trust issues with Worker Bee #4. And speaking of which, who is Worker Bee #4."

"Sounds like she was using a code name," says Callie.

"I wonder if worker bee #4 is Ida, the assistant beekeeper," I surmise.

"Might be," says Callie. "Maybe that's why she used 'worker bee' as a code word."

"You might be right," I say.

"Is that all she wrote?"

I turn a few more pages. "Here's something ... *'today I almost got caught'* ... and again, that's the only thing she wrote on this page."

"Caught doing what?" the cat asks.

I shrug. "That's all it says. But, maybe she got caught looking for evidence that the medical center is doing something crooked."

"Anything else?"

Flipping to the next page, I stop. "Oh my gosh …"

"What?" Callie demands.

"Dora wrote … *'the doctor is a crook'* … "

"What doctor?"

"Dr. Napier, I'll bet," I tell the Calico, scanning the page. "And a few lines down, on the same page this time, she wrote, *'using bee venom for shady reasons'* … and *'doctor making false promises'* … "

"Girl, that sounds like the bee venom facials don't work," says the cat. "The doctor is lying to his clients."

"I get the feeling Dr. Napier is doing a lot worse," I say, flipping a few more pages. "Three months ago, she wrote, *'something not right about the honey spray'* … "

"What honey spray?" Callie asks.

Recalling my conversations with Mrs. Post and Mrs. DuFault, I say, "I think it's the spray the housekeeping staff sprayed in the client's rooms. They didn't like the spray but the housekeeper kept spraying it."

"Why would the housekeeper do that?"

"I don't know," I say. "But I wonder if the honey spray, somehow, makes the clients lose their memory."

"So they won't remember giving money to the charity," surmises Callie.

"Oh no …" I say, my heart slamming as I read. "On an entry dated last month, Dora wrote … *'doctor threatened me today'* … and …"

"And what, sis?" demands Callie.

Swallowing, I say, "Dora wrote … *'doctor advised me to be careful or something bad might happen to me'* … and that's the last entry."

Callie says, "Dr. Napier killed Dora Butler… "

Nodding, I say, "Now I have to prove it."

# Chapter 21

"You want to … what?" asks my boss, Marty, staring at me like I've grown a third arm, or perhaps a second nose. I would say Marty is looking at me like I've lost my mind, but he usually looks at me like that, askance and askew, but the look he's giving me now is different.

Marty's eyes are bugged and he's turning a sickly shade of purple, which is worrisome, because normally, when he's upset with me, he turns fire hydrant red.

Clearing my throat, I sit straighter in the chair, positioned on the opposite side of Marty's large desk, which is strewn with files, documents, books, and various office products—a stapler, a pen holder, rubber bands, and a three-hole punch machine.

"I want to go undercover at the Bee Well Medical Center," I say, trying to keep my voice firm and confident like I'm sure my mentor—Vivian Thomas, the award-winning foreign correspondent—would do if she were pitching an idea to her editor. Really, I'm shaking in my boots, even though I'm not wearing boots. It's far too hot for boots on an island in the Caribbean. Actually, I'm wearing a pair of pink gladiator sandals that pair nicely with my mint green seersucker wrap dress, so I suppose I should say, I'm shaking in my sandals.

"Why on earth do you want to do that?"

"I want to prove that Dora Butler was murdered by the medical center's founder, Dr. Napier."

"What are you talking about?" demands Marty, scowling at me. "Dora Butler's death was accidental. She pumped herself full of bee venom to look younger and ended up a corpse."

"Well, yes, that is what the police think, however … "

"However?"

I take a deep breath. "I have reason to believe Dora's death was not an accident, but homicide."

"You have reason to believe?" Marty snorts, the leather chair creaking as he leans back. "And just what are the reasons you believe?"

Deciding not to be deterred by Marty's doubt, I say, "Well, for one, both Dora's friend, Marlo, and her niece, Samantha, think she was murdered."

"Right," says Marty. "You mentioned that in your follow-up articles. But, neither had proof. It was just speculation based on conversations they claimed to have had with Dora."

"True," I concede. "We have to take their word that Dora told them she suspected something shady was going on at the medical center. So that's why I dug a little deeper …"

Eyes narrowed, Marty says, "Go on …"

"I spoke with Dora's neighbor," I tell Marty. "And she saw Dora arguing with a man one rainy night. Dora and the man, who was tall and thin, left in a car, and the next day Dora was found dead on the beach."

"Who's the tall, thin guy?"

"I believe the man is one of Dora's coworkers," I say. "I found out that he drove Dora to the Bee Well Day Spa. Based on CCTV footage, Dora and the tall, thin coworker went into the day spa, but only the man came out. He drove to the marina and took a ferry, but I'm not sure to what island, though I suspect he went to Bee Island, where the medical center is located."

"Was Dr. Napier the coworker who argued with Dora?"

"I don't think so," I say. "Dr. Napier is short and squat."

Marty leans forward. "So you think what? The tall, thin coworker drove Dora to the day spa where Dr. Napier was waiting to kill her?"

"Again, I'm not sure," I say. "Dora's friend Marlo thinks an assistant beekeeper who works at the center, her name is Ida, killed Dora, but I'm not sure about that now. I think it's more plausible that Dr. Napier told the tall, thin man to kill Dora."

"And why would Dr. Napier want Dora dead?" asks Marty. "What's this shady business going on that she supposedly found out about?"

"I'm not quite sure," I admit. "But I think Dr. Napier is tricking his clients into giving large donations of money to his charity, which I don't think exists, called Save the Bees."

"How is he tricking the clients?"

"I believe he's using the bee venom to, somehow, convince them to donate and then make them forget what happened during their stay at the medical center."

Marty scratches his chin. "That's a bold claim."

"But I think it's true," I say. "A few days ago, Dora's niece gave me permission to look for clues in Dora's house. I located a journal hidden beneath Dora's bed. In the journal, Dora wrote about the doctor being a crook, using the bee venom for shady reasons, and threatening to kill her."

Marty blows out a breath. "If what Dora wrote in the diary is true—"

"I believe it is," I say, trying to temper my excitement and hope because I'm not sure Marty is convinced, but I think he might be. "That's why I want to go undercover as a client at the Bee Well Medical Center. I think that will be my best chance to find evidence that proves Dr. Napier killed Dora or had something to do with her murder."

Rubbing his eyes, Marty says, "Sophia, I'm sure I don't have to remind you that you've tried to do sting operations before and you've never been successful."

Marty doesn't have to remind me.

My last three attempts to pull off a sting operation failed, and each time, I almost got killed. Nevertheless, and despite the odds stacked against me, I say, "I'm aware of that but I think I have to try."

Folding his arms across his chest, Marty looks less than convinced.

I continue, "A grave injustice is being perpetuated by the founder of the medical center and it would be a horrible tragedy if I don't try to uncover the heinous corruption."

"Sophia, you're laying it on a bit thick."

Sheepish, I say, "Oh, sorry … "

Marty exhales. "It's not a bad idea … "

"But?" I prompt.

"I'm worried," he admits. "It could be dangerous."

"I know," I say, sensing that Marty might finally be on board with my idea. "But I know I can do it."

"Just be careful," Marty advises. "If you're right about this medical center, then it means this doctor has killed before. And he probably won't hesitate to kill again … "

# Chapter 22

The driver opens the back door of the Bentley sedan and waits for me to get out.

Callie is also waiting, saying, "Girl, why are you just sitting here? Get out so we can put this sting into operation and find out who killed Dora Butler."

Nodding, I take a deep breath. "Right …"

But I don't move.

Because I can't. Okay, that's not true. Technically, I can move. That is to say, I have full mobility of my limbs and I can use my muscles to stand and my legs to walk.

However, I don't want to get out of the car, which isn't even mine. The luxury vehicle is a rental, provided by the publisher of the *Palmchat Gazette*, Leo Bronson, Vivian's husband, who comes from a family of billionaires. When the black Bentley arrived at my apartment to "collect" me, as the driver put it, I didn't know what to think. I've never even sat in a Bentley before, let alone been driven around in one as though it was no big deal, something I did every day.

Then again, as a privileged West Indian heiress, being chauffeured would be an everyday occurrence.

And since the sting operation calls for me to portray a young, wealthy socialite, I have to act the part. After all, the sting was my big idea. I convinced Marty to let me go undercover as a client at the Bee Well Medical Center to look for clues in the murder of Dora Butler. Once Marty got on board, he called Vivian, and my mentor thought it was a great idea. She even called me with tips and tricks on carrying out a successful stealth operation.

I assured Marty and Vivian that I was up for the task.

But I felt that way a week ago.

Now that I'm faced with the daunting goal I need to accomplish, I'm anxious and worried. I don't want to let Marty and Vivian down. If this sting operation fails, I don't know if I'll get another chance to prove myself as an intrepid investigative reporter.

"Miss ...?" prompts the chauffeur, frowning.

"Girl, if you don't get out of this car ... " warns the Calico.

"Okay, okay," I mumble, gathering her in my arms, something she's only allowing because she's playing the part of my pampered housecat. "I'm getting out."

Standing on wobbly knees, clutching Callie for dear life, I thank the driver with a nod of my head, then take a deep breath and—

"Relax your hold, sis," complains Callie. "You're going to squeeze all nine of my lives out of me."

"Sorry ... " I say.

"Sorry?" asks the driver, giving me an attentive frown.

"Oh, um," I say, then clear my throat. "What I meant was ... can you please get my things?"

"Of course, miss," says the driver, hurrying to the trunk of the car.

"Well, here goes nothing ..." I whisper to the cat as I stare at the Bee Well Medical Center, an imposing three-story colonial mansion nestled into lush, verdant rainforest. On the hour-long ferry to the private island, I calmed my nerves by studying the center's website, which features a photo of the center. Despite knowing beforehand what the facility looks like, I'm still unprepared for how looming and intimidating it seems.

Once I head through those tall, wide orangewood doors, there will be no turning back. The sting operation will begin. While pretending to be Sophia Cartier, I'll have to sneak around, searching for proof that some sort of malfeasance taking place in the center got her killed.

Suddenly, I feel rooted to the spot as Marty's dire warning comes back to me.

*If you're right about this medical center, then it means this doctor has killed before. And he probably won't hesitate to kill again.*

"What's wrong, sis?" asks Callie.

Shaking my head, I glance at her and whisper, "Nothing. I'm just a bit nervous."

"Well, don't worry," says Callie. "I'm not a scaredy cat and if anyone tries to hurt you, I'll just scratch their eyes right out of their head!"

Giggling, I tell her, "Good to know."

Ahead, the wooden doors start to open, and my heart starts to slam. "This is it," I whisper to Callie as I head down the wide, paved stone path. The chauffeur follows behind me with my luggage.

"It'll be fine, girl," says the cat. "You're Sophia Cartier now, so act like it."

"Right ..." I murmur, taking my time to navigate the ten steps up to the expansive porch that travels the length of the building. As I take the final few steps to the doors, they open wide.

My racing heart drops into my stomach as my mouth goes dry. I glance up at the staff member, dressed in crisp white linen scrubs, who stands in the massive doorway.

"Welcome to the Bee Well Medical Center ..." says the tall, thin man.

# Chapter 23

"You think that tall, thin man who greeted us killed Dora?" asks Callie, stretched out on the hibiscus-and-palm printed duvet.

Pacing around the four-post king-sized bed in the center of my suite, I bite my bottom lip. "Well, I'm certain he's the guy Dora's neighbor saw her arguing with on the porch in the rain. But, I'm not sure if he murdered Dora. He's still a suspect, but so is Dr. Napier, who may have killed Dora, or arranged her death."

"Girl, he looks like a killer," says the Calico.

I'm inclined to agree, shuddering involuntarily as I recall meeting Dora's tall, thin coworker.

Despite the balmy, tropical atmosphere, I was chilled to the bone as I stared at him, disconcerted by his gaunt, skeletal face, pale, sickly complexion, deep-set eyes, and thin lips, which drew back into a grim smile.

"Welcome to the Bee Well Medical Center …" he'd said, his voice deep and raspy, sort of like how a monster hiding under a bed would sound. "My name is Ransbleen Reiss. I am the General Manager and your host. On behalf of Dr. Napier, we are delighted to have you here."

Trying not to cower beneath his imposing gaze, I swallowed my fear and forced myself to begin my ruse as Sophia Cartier, the pampered West Indian heiress.

Stopping at the foot of the bed, I glance at the cat. "You know, I can't imagine how terrifying it must have been for Dora, arguing with him on a dark and stormy night."

"Girl, she's braver than me," says Callie, licking her paw. "And you know I'm not a scaredy cat but there is no way I would have gotten into the car and gone anywhere with that ghoul."

"Unfortunately, that's what Dora did," I say.

"And that was the last thing she did," says Callie.

"That's what I have to prove," I say, crossing my arms.

"Speaking of proving it," says Callie. "What's the next step?"

Exhaling, I walk to the sitting area and pick up a silk-covered folder. "Well, here's my schedule …"

"What do they have you doing?" Callie asks, leaping down from the bed and trotting over toward me.

Opening the folder, I glance at the words printed on elegant lambskin paper. "In an hour, I have a garden reception for new clients."

"What are you going to wear?" the cat asks, jumping up onto the coffee table.

"Luckily," I say, smiling, "Vivian gave me a generous budget so I have some super cute dresses. I think I'm going to wear this lovely yellow sundress, in honor of honey and bees, you know?"

"Sounds good, sis," says Callie. "While you're at the reception, I'm going to see what I can find out from the animals on the property. The lizards, birds, and … well, the bees … might have some tea about this place."

An hour later, in my sunny, frilly frock, I'm sitting in a wonderful rose garden with four other women, all of them much older, and wondering why I'm there, but they seem to have accepted I'm interested in pre-prevention, as it's never too early to start.

"Hopefully, dear, we'll all leave here looking like you," says a sixty-something wealthy businesswoman named Dandy Descoteaux.

"Oh, we should be so lucky!" says Ethel Oliveria, a bubbly, giggly heiress with the heart of a pre-teen girl, clapping her hands.

"With what they're charging us, they better have a fountain of youth at this place," grumbles Georgia Troy, who confessed to being in her fifties and has a billionaire husband.

"I hope the treatments are safe," says Blanche, frowning as she wrings her wrinkled hands. "I don't want to find out, at sixty-two years old, that I'm allergic to honey. And can you imagine getting stung by a bee and swelling up like a balloon?"

"I think we'll all bee okay ..." I say, chuckling. "Get it?"

The four older women stare at me with expressions ranging from confusion to despair to suspicion.

"Bee okay ..." I repeat, emphasizing the word 'bee.' "You know, because we're at the Bee Well Medical Center and we'll be okay ... bee and be are homophones."

"Homophones ..." repeats Georgia.

Nodding, I say, "Words that sound alike but have different meanings."

"Not to change the subject ..." says Ethel.

"Please do," says Dandy.

"Have you heard anything about the staff?" Ethel asks, eyes wide as she glances at us.

"The staff?" asks Georgia, frowning. "What do you mean? What would we have heard about the staff?"

I'm wondering the same thing but pretending not to care as I listen intently.

Ethel says, "Well, we're supposed to have our own personal spa attendant and two housekeepers for our rooms, but how can that be when one of the housekeepers was let go."

"Let go?" asks Dandy. "When?"

"Better yet, why?" asks Georgia.

Voice lowered, Ethel says, "Apparently, she was stealing from the guests."

"Stealing from the guests?" I repeat, wondering if the housekeeper might have been the coworker Dora was referring to when she told Winifred East about a coworker who'd threatened her. I'd assumed it might be Ida, the assistant beekeeper, but maybe not. Although, stealing from guests doesn't seem like the sort of shady shenanigans that Dora was trying to expose. Based on her diary entries, Dora was suspicious of the center's doctors and their treatments. I doubt the housekeeper had anything to do with that.

"Ladies ... welcome to the new client initiation reception ..."

The deep, reptilian rasp of Ransbleen Reiss slithers through the air, commanding my attention as I focus on the towering, lanky man. Again I shudder and try not to arouse his skepticism as he stands a few feet away from us, reciting his introductory message.

"It is my great pleasure to welcome you to the Bee Well Medical Center. Again, I am Ransbleen Reiss, the General Manager, and I am honored to introduce you to the man who created and founded the center, Dr. Fernando Napier."

Dr. Napier appears, a short, rotund man with a dark piercing gaze. He wears a white coat with his name embroidered above the left top pocket while keeping both hands in the deep, wide lower pockets. Staring at him, I can't help wondering if I'm looking at Dora Butler's killer. Did those hands he's hiding inject Dora with a lethal dose of bee venom and then scatter dead bees on her corpse?

After a smattering of polite applause, Dr. Napier begins. "I am thrilled to introduce you to our unique and specialized approach to facial treatments, which harnesses the incredible natural benefits of bee products. At the Bee Well Medical Center, we believe in the power of nature and its ability to rejuvenate and heal. Our treatments are crafted with the finest ingredients from the beehive, including bee pollen, beeswax, and bee venom."

A jolt passes through me as Dr. Napier pauses to look at us, a strange glint in his beady little eyes, one I can't read, but which seems to be somewhat malicious. Next to him, Ransbleen Reiss also stares at us, his gaze piercing, almost menacing. Again, I can definitely imagine him as Dora's killer.

"Bee products have been used for centuries for their therapeutic properties," explains Dr. Napier. "Through extensive research, I have been able to harness their potential to create innovative and effective facial treatments. Our team of skilled professionals is dedicated to providing you with personalized care and treatments that cater to your individual needs. We are committed to ensuring that your experience with us is not only effective but also relaxing and rejuvenating. And now, with more information regarding our bee products, I give you our apiarist, Dr. Peter Jones."

Another man appears, loping around the bushes, and stands next to Dr. Napier. He's dressed casually, in jeans and a short-sleeved plaid cotton shirt, and has a head of wiry, salt-and-pepper hair, like Albert Einstein. Rangy and stooped over, Dr. Jones glances at us with a furtive glare, his gaze a bit unfocused, which may be because the pupil of his right eye is trained on us while the other seems to float, untethered, in the white sclera of his left eye.

"Bee pollen is rich in vitamins, minerals, and amino acids," says Dr. Jones. "It is a powerhouse for nourishing and revitalizing your skin. Beeswax provides a natural barrier that locks in moisture and protects your skin from environmental damage. Bee venom, often referred to as nature's Botox, stimulates collagen production and helps to smooth and firm the skin, giving you a more youthful and radiant appearance."

Dr. Jones' information about bee venom reminds me of what Samantha Butler said about her aunt, how Dora's skin was youthful and supple. And from looking at her photo, it was clear Dora didn't need to stimulate collagen production. Her appearance was already radiant.

More than ever, I'm convinced she was murdered.

And one of the men standing a few feet from me might have killed her.

# Chapter 24

"So, that's the tour!" says Suzie, my PSA, personal spa assistant, an energetic woman wearing crisp, pristine lavender scrubs. "I hope you enjoyed it!!"

"Yes, I really did!" I say, which is true.

Two hours ago, Suzie showed up at my door, following my scrumptious breakfast — fruit, and toast with fresh honey and lemon-and-honey infused tea — introducing herself and announcing that she would give me a tour of the facilities.

Callie was still sleeping, so I left the Calico curled up on the bed and joined Suzie, who took me around the massive medical center complex. We piled into a golf cart and Suzie drove down the wide honeycomb-shaped paths, doing a running commentary as we visited the gardens, the lab where the serums are made by dedicated chemists, the medical ward where I'll be receiving the treatments, and the admin building.

"Any questions?" asks Suzie, standing outside the double doors to my luxury suite.

"Um, yes," I say. "I was hoping we might get to meet some of the beekeepers. A friend of mine who came here said she was able to meet an assistant beekeeper named Ida ..."

Suzie says, "The beekeepers are extremely busy—as a bee, ha ha ..."

"Ha ha ..." I say, faking a laugh.

"However, due to their busy schedules, there won't be any official opportunities to meet them, but should you see a beekeeper on our grounds, you are more than welcome to say hello."

Nodding, I say, "I'll do that. Maybe I can say hello to Ida."

"Well, that won't be possible," says Suzie. "Ida no longer works here."

Disappointed, I say, "Oh, that's too bad."

"Actually, it's good," says Suzie, voice lowered. "Ida was fired last year after she was suspected of stealing bee hives."

"That's terrible," I say. "So, she hasn't worked here since last year."

Suzie says, "Right. She made a real stink about her termination. Said she was being framed and all that. Threatened to sue. But a week later, she was on a plane back to Australia, where she was from."

"Is she still in Australia?" I ask.

Suzie says, "Yes. She has a beekeeping YouTube channel about her adventures on a bee farm in Sydney. It's quite informative and entertaining."

"I'll have to check it out," I remark.

"So, anything else?"

"Um, yes," I say. "I was wondering who my nurse will be?"

"Oh, I'm not sure," says Suzie. "But I can find out and let you know."

"I was told to request Dora Butler," I say.

Suzie's face falls. "Oh, I'm sorry to tell you this, but ... Dora Butler passed away."

"Oh, that's awful!" I say, feigning ignorance. "Do you know what happened? Was she ill?"

Her gaze furtive, Suzie looks over her shoulder, then steps closer to me. "Well, I shouldn't gossip, but the rumor is she injected herself with bee venom, that she'd stolen, into her face to look younger but ended up poisoning herself."

"That's terrible," I say.

"Yeah, but ..."

"But?" I prompt, hoping to get more information.

Suzie shakes her head. "Well, it's odd because Dora was a nurse, and she would know how much bee venom to use or not to use so it's weird that she accidentally poisoned herself."

Suzie has a good point, one I hadn't thought of, but I say, "Maybe she decided to risk it for the sake of eternal youth."

"But, that's weird, too," says Suzie. "Dora didn't need these bee venom treatments. Her skin was flawless."

I give a disinterested murmur, but I'm not surprised by Suzie's assessment of Dora's skin. It's more confirmation that Dora didn't inject herself with stolen bee venom to look younger.

"Okay so, dinner is at eight," Suzie reminds me. "See you then and enjoy your leisure time!"

# Chapter 25

"What did you have for dinner?" I ask Callie as we stroll along the walking path back to my suite.

The sun has set, leaving behind a sky streaked with orange, pink, and gold. It's a lovely, balmy evening, and even though I'm on a sting operation, I'm enjoying the chirping insects, tree frogs, and fragrant breeze. The night sounds are a nice addition following the meal I finished half an hour ago. Ethel, Dandy, Georgia, and I joined each other for a scrumptious dinner—Jerk sea bass, mashed plantains, and steamed greens. For dessert, we were treated to honeycomb ice cream.

Trotting next to me, Callie says, "Fresh tuna. It was excellent!"

"Glad to hear that," I say. "I told the staff it was your favorite."

"Girl, they may be stone-cold killers," says the cat. "But they have good customer service. They took me to a nice area near the beach and I was able to climb a palm tree and then I laid on the sand and slept."

"Sounds like you had a great time," I say, following the path through a dense cluster of tropical bushes.

"What about you?" asks the cat.

"Dinner was great, but I couldn't concentrate."

"Girl, why not?"

"Well, I was thinking about what Suzie told me about Ida, the assistant beekeeper," I say, continuing down the path, rounding a corner.

"Girl, don't be upset that Ida doesn't work here anymore," advises the cat. "I know you wanted to question her, but I think Marlo was wrong about her being the murderer. Obviously, it's probably Dr. Napier."

"Right, right," I agree. "But, it occurred to me that Ida couldn't have killed Dora. After she was fired, she moved back to Australia. And she denied stealing bee hives."

"Of course, she wouldn't admit it, sis," says the cat.

"No, but ... I'm wondering if Dora was wrong about her," I say. "Maybe Ida didn't have a motive because she didn't do anything wrong. Maybe she was framed."

"Or, maybe Dora got Ida fired," says Callie. "Dora might have thought Ida stole bee hives, then told Dr. Napier, who fired Ida ... which would give her a motive."

"But, Ida doesn't have opportunity," I say. "She's been in Australia for the past year. I found her YouTube channel. She uploaded a new video yesterday. And I discovered that she was doing a live Q and A on her channel the day that Dora was last seen alive."

"She can't be in two places at the same time," says the cat.

"Right," I say. "So, we can take Ida off the suspect list. But that leaves—"

"Girl, do you smell that?"

Slowing to a halt, I sniff the air. "Smell what?" I ask, picking up a faint scent of rose, jasmine, hibiscus, and—

"Honey ..." says Callie, padding slowly toward a large cluster of Oleander trees used as a natural privacy wall between the premium bungalows. "Girl, come take a look at this ... "

"Take a look at what?" I ask, angling off the path and closer to the wall of Oleander trees.

"Peep between the trees …"

Stepping onto the grass, I lean toward the Oleander trees and peer between the thin leaves and fuchsia flowers. Roughly fifteen feet away, on the porch of the premium bungalow, is a housekeeping cart made of bamboo. The housekeeper, however, is nowhere to be found, but the bungalow door is open, so I think the room must be receiving room service.

"I think the honey smell is coming from inside that bungalow," says the cat.

"Interesting …" I whisper, thinking of what Mrs. DuFault and Mrs. Post, Candace's friend who's not really her friend, told me about honey-smelling freshener sprayed in their rooms.

"Girl, more like nauseating," says Callie. "I'm about to gag."

"Hold it down … " I tell the cat. "I'm going to check out that housekeeping cart and see if the honey spray is there. I think there's something weird about that spray."

"You think it causes memory loss?" asks the cat.

"Possibly," I say. "But I won't know unless I get a sample of it."

"Good idea," says the cat, licking her paw. "You can ask Officer Good-looking to test it."

"Okay, cover me," I tell the cat. "If someone is coming, then—"

"I'll caterwaul like I did that time when you stepped on my tail," says Callie.

"You know I didn't mean that," I say, giving the cat a look for reminding me of an inadvertent mistake I made.

"Just get going, sis," says Callie. "And be careful."

"I'll *bee* careful," I promise, giggling. "Get it? I'll *bee* careful … bee … because we're at the Bee Well—"

"Girl, this is no time for silly puns," says Callie.

"You're right," I tell the cat, forcing myself to stop hesitating.

Carefully, I step through the Oleander bushes, pushing past the leaves, and stepping onto the grass on the opposite side. My heart slams as I tiptoe toward the porch, making sure to keep a look out around me. Hurrying up the stairs, I walk onto the gleaming wooden plank porch and slink over to the open doors of the bungalow. Peeking around the doorframe, I glance inside. The furnishings and décor are expensive and elegant, even more so than my suite, naturally.

During the dinner with Dandy, Ethel, and Georgia, I learned that Dandy has a suite, like me, but Ethel and Georgia have bungalows, which are the most expensive accommodations at the medical center.

Biting my bottom lip, I stare past the foyer, down the hall, and into the living area, where a maid is at the back of the room, dusting. Quickly, I dash over to the housekeeping cart parked inside the door. Quickly, I scan the contents. On the top of the cart are cleaning products, and that's where I find a pressurized aerosol can that says ROOM SANITIZER.

Lowering my head, I sniff the nozzle.

My pulse starts to race.

There's a faint trace of honey smell.

I stare at the can, wondering, thinking back on what Mrs. Post and Mrs. DuFault told me about housekeepers spraying a honey air freshener in their rooms. Did the air freshener cause some sort of memory loss? Was it sprayed in rooms so the clients wouldn't remember donating large amounts of money to the Save the Bees charity?

Well, that's what I need to find out.

I reach for the can and—

"What are you doing, Ms. Cartier?"

# Chapter 26

I freeze.

Then thaw, and then freeze again, my heart slamming, my mind in a panic at the looming presence behind me.

"Ms. Cartier ...?"

The sinister, rasping voice of Ransbleen Reiss snakes around me like a slithering snake, making me shudder. Part of me wants to take off running, but another part, the part that's telling me to remember I'm in the middle of a sting operation, is struggling to come up with an answer to the general manager's question.

Clearing my throat, I turn.

Ransbleen stands too close as he peers down at me with a grim grin. Startled, I step back, and then say, "Oh, you scared me ..."

"The guilty flee when no man pursues," says Ransbleen, eyes narrowed as he gives me a suspicious glare.

"I'm sorry?" I ask, unfamiliar with the phrase.

"Nothing," he says, shaking his head. "Something my grandmother used to say. May I ask, are you lost? This isn't your suite."

"Oh, I um ..." Wary of rambling, I let out a quick break. "I was looking for ... stain remover."

"Stain remover?"

"Yes, stain remover," I say, realizing I sound ridiculous but I've committed to this excuse so I have to sell it, or at least see it through. "I discovered a stain on one of my dresses and as I was walking back to my room, following dinner, I saw this housekeeping cart and I wanted to ask the housekeeper, but I didn't see her so I thought I would check the cart to see—"

"This is not stain remover," says Ransbleen, snatching the can from me. "It clearly says room sanitizer."

"Oh, yes, it does ... " I make a show of staring at the can, as though this is the first time I've seen it. "I didn't pay attention ... well, I'll be going."

"Ms. Cartier," says Ransbleen, returning the can to the housekeeping cart. "In the future, if you need anything, like stain remover, you are to contact your PSA."

"Right," I say. "Well, good night ..."

"I'll escort you back to your room," says Ransbleen.

"Oh, that won't be necessary," I say, anxious to get away from him.

"I think it will be very necessary," says Ransbleen, placing a hand beneath my elbow and guiding me off the porch, down the steps, and onto the path leading to the main walkway.

"Oh, well, okay, if you insist ..."

"I do," he says, his tone curt and flat.

"How kind of you," I reply, though I doubt he's being gentlemanly. I'm sure Ransbleen wants to make sure I get to my suite without any more detours.

I'm also sure he was skeptical of my story about the stain remover, which means I need to be extra careful around him from now on. I don't need him to develop any doubts about me. I can't have one of my main suspects suspicious of me.

"Ms. Cartier ... "

"Yes?" I answer, fighting apprehension as we traverse a narrow path, shrouded in darkness, through a tunnel of trees. A balmy breeze rustles the leaves, fooling me into thinking there's something dark and sinister watching me behind the branches.

"It has come to my attention," says Ransbleen, "that you inquired about a nurse who used to work here named Dora Butler."

Swallowing my wariness, and hoping we'll arrive at my suite soon, I say, "I was told she was very competent and to request her services, but I was informed that she ... passed away."

"What happened to Dora Butler was unfortunate ..."

Ransbleen pauses. There's only the sound of our footsteps on concrete. I can't help thinking that I'm walking next to a killer. And that Ransbleen might be recalling, at this moment, how he murdered Dora Butler.

"However," continues Ransbleen. "Dora Butler was an unstable woman obsessed with youth and that obsession drove her to commit reprehensible acts which led to her own demise."

"That is ... unfortunate," I say, but I'm thinking that it's also a lie. Several people have told me, and I've seen with my own eyes, that Dora had fantastic skin. She wasn't obsessed with youth.

"Your suite is ahead," says Ransbleen, guiding me around a stand of palm trees, where we walk out of the dark path and into the illumination of the main building. Here the trees and walkways are festooned with lights, which put me at ease.

Moments later, at the door to my suite, Ransbleen says, "Ms. Cartier, if you will permit me, might I extend a word of advice?"

"Certainly," I say.

"Normally, someone so young as yourself does not visit our center," he says. "I hope that you have not become obsessed with youth and beauty as vanity is a grave sin and sin, of course, leads to death, as Dora Butler found out. Have a good evening."

I manage a wan smile as Ransbleen walks away, wondering if he's kidding about me having a good evening. All I'm going to have this evening is fears of impending nightmares after that dire warning about vanity, sin, and death.

Exhaling, I step into my suite.

"Girl, where have you been?" demands Callie, standing in the middle of the bed.

Closing the door behind me, I say, "Well, you're one to talk. What happened to you? What happened to warning me if someone was coming? That crypt keeper Ransbleen caught me snooping around the housekeeping cart."

"Girl, as soon as you walked away," says the cat, licking her paw, "I saw a mouse, so I went after him."

"You went after a mouse?" I shake my head as I bend down to take off my shoes.

"I'm a cat," says the Calico. "I chase mice. Sue me. Better yet, give me the tea about the housekeeping cart."

"Well," I say, dropping down onto the bed. "I think I found the honey spray that Candace's friend and Mrs. DuFault said was sprayed in their rooms."

"Did you get it so Officer Cuetee can have it tested?"

"I was about to but then Ransbleen caught me," I say. "I gave him some story about thinking it was stain remover, which he didn't believe, but he definitely didn't want me anywhere near the honey spray."

"You think he's been telling the housekeepers to spray the rooms?" asks Callie.

Staring at the ceiling, I say, "It's possible. They obviously take instructions from him. The way I see it, so far, is that Ransbleen told the housekeepers to spray the honey air freshener which causes memory loss so the clients wouldn't remember giving those large donations."

"And maybe Dora Butler found out what he was doing," says the cat.

I sit up. "Dora probably threatened to expose Ransbleen's plot ... and he killed her."

# Chapter 27

"So what's the plan for today," asks Callie, lying on the divan in the sitting area, making biscuits on one of the accent pillows.

"Now that breakfast is over," I say, glancing at the remnants of my morning meal—fruit and yogurt, drizzled with fresh honey, and honey lavender tea, which by the way would go great with glazed plum donut holes. "I have to get ready for my first treatment."

"Treatment?" The cat pauses her kneading to stare at me. "Girl, don't tell me you're going to let these psychos inject you with bee venom!"

"Relax," I say, finishing my tea. "I'm having a beeswax facial. It should be harmless."

"And what if it's not?" demands Callie.

"I think the only thing I have to worry about is that honey spray," I say. "Speaking of which, I need to smuggle a can out of this place."

"And what if you do?" asks Callie. "And what if there is some chemical in the spray that causes memory loss? How will you prove that Dr. Napier put the chemical in the spray."

"Proving that will be a problem," I acknowledge.

"Lucky you have me to help you," says the cat. "While you're getting beeswax slathered and smeared all over your face, I'm going to take a look around and see if I can find out anything."

"Sounds like a plan," I tell the cat before I let her out of the French doors that open to the rear terrace of the suite.

Thirty minutes later, following a luxurious shower, I dress in comfy leisurewear then head to the medical ward, an expansive Colonial building decorated with rattan and bamboo furniture, with barkcloth, jute, and sisal accents, strategically placed palm trees, and colors of the island, aqua, tan, and green.

After checking in with the receptionist, I'm greeted by an assistant who guides me down a series of hallways to the room where I'll have my first treatment, not that I'm looking forward to having beeswax slathered across my face. My nerves aren't shot but I'm anxious to put my plan into action, which is questioning the nurse esthetician about Dora Butler.

The assistant helps me put on a smock to protect my outfit, then invites me to sit down in the spa chair in the center of the room. After helping me get comfortable, the assistant dims the lights and presses a few buttons near the door before closing it. Alone in the room, I take a deep breath, taking in the relaxing fragrance of jasmine and hibiscus.

But I'm not relaxed.

My mind is churning, rehashing my theories about what might have happened to Dora Butler. So far, I think Dora discovered that the honey room fragrance was causing clients to have memory loss. She obviously suspected Ransbleen Reiss and confronted him. It's possible their argument on her porch that rainy night was about the general manager's malfeasance.

One thing I'm unsure about is how Ransbleen killed Dora, considering that he drove her to the day spa, they both went inside, but only Ransbleen exited. Then, he took a ferry from St. Mateo, probably to Bee Island. I'm wondering, did he kill Dora in the day spa, then leave her body there, travel to Bee Island, then return to St. Mateo to leave her corpse on the beach?

Staring at the palmetto-shaped ceiling fan swirling lazily above me, I start to think it makes sense that Ransbleen went to Bee Island to get the dead bees he needed to make it appear that Dora accidentally poisoned herself in a misguided attempt to look younger.

A soft knock on the door startles me from my ruminations.

The door opens and a petite woman with a blonde pixie cut peeks around it, smiling. "Ready for your beeswax facial?"

Nodding, I say, "I've been looking forward to it."

"Great!" She says, walking into the room. "First things first, I'm Aria, your certified nurse esthetician and I'm excited to give you this wonderful facial."

Humming a jaunty tune, Aria walks to the overhead cabinets, opens them, and takes out several bottles and jars, filled with, I'm assuming, bee by-products she'll use to whip up the beeswax facial ingredients.

"So let me tell you a bit about beeswax while I prepare your facial," says Aria as she removes a few bowls from a lower cabinet, and then arranges them in a line.

In less than ten minutes, while mixing ingredients in a bowl with a pestle, Aria explains how beeswax is a substance secreted by worker honeybees to build their honeycombs, that it's great for dry and sensitive skin, and is wonderful as a moisturizer because it acts as an emollient, softening your skin and restoring your skin's natural lipid layer.

"As I perform the facial," says Aria, "you'll notice that the beeswax will create a protective barrier on top of your skin that will help your skin to heal. It will keep moisture from getting out, which is important, because dry skin can prevent your skin from repairing itself, and the beeswax will prevent irritants from breaking past the skin barrier."

"Impressive," I say.

"So, tell me, how did you hear about the Bee Well Medical Center?" asks Aria.

"I was referred by Felice DuFault," I say, which technically is sorta, kinda true.

"Mrs. DuFault," says Aria, nodding. "Lovely woman. I gave her a honeycomb foot scrub."

"She told me to get the beeswax facial," I say. "And she recommended another procedure that she had done by a nurse named Dora Butler … do you know what procedure that is? And how can I book with Dora?"

"Oh I'm sorry to tell you this, but …" Aria pauses, continuing to mix the facial ingredients.

"But?"

"Dora passed away," says Aria.

"Oh, how terrible," I say, pretending to be clueless. "Was she ill?"

"No, she was found dead on the beach," says Aria, shuddering. "So awful. It was in the *Palmchat Gazette*. That's where I read about it."

"I don't read the paper," I say quickly, feeling both worried and a little proud about my story. "But, um, what happened to her? Did she have a sunstroke, or—"

"I'm not sure," says Aria, facing me. "Apparently she was found covered in dead bees. And, Dr. Napier doesn't want the staff discussing Dora, but apparently, she stole some bee hives, which I find crazy, but now I guess it makes sense."

"What makes sense?" I ask.

"You know that theory about accusing other people of doing something when you're the one doing it?" Aria asks. "Like how people who cheat always accuse others of cheating?"

Nodding, I say, "Yes, I have heard about that."

"Well, a month or so before Dora died," says Aria. "I overheard Dora and one of the housekeepers arguing."

"She argued with a housekeeper?" I ask, wondering why the information seems familiar.

"Dora accused the housekeeper of stealing bee hives and selling them," says Aria. "But, I guess the truth was that Dora was the real thief. Maybe."

"Maybe?" I prompt, sensing some doubt from Aria.

"I can't imagine Dora stealing bee hives," admits Aria. "Which is not to say that she didn't do it, because people can fool you. But, the housekeeper she accused was very sketchy."

"In what way?"

"I can't think of anything specific," Aria says. "I hate to say this but she looked suspicious. She was always lurking around. The other housekeepers complained that she was never on her post and took long breaks. Dr. Napier got rid of her, but a few weeks ago, Ransbleen asked Napier to bring her back on staff. She's his cousin, so Ransbleen is looking out for her."

"Interesting," I say.

"And, since there was no proof that she stole anything, I guess Napier relented," says Aria. "I wish I could remember her name, but I only met her a few times. Anyway, part of me thinks Dora was right about the housekeeper. Part of me thinks Ransbleen's cousin did steal the bee hives."

# Chapter 28

After my beeswax facial, which was wonderful and refreshing, leaving me feeling and looking rejuvenated and hydrated, Aria escorted me to a relaxing room where I spent time dozing and letting my mind roam.

But now, thirty minutes later, I'm walking down the dimly lit hallway, contemplating what Aria told me about Dora's argument with a housekeeper. I was wondering why the information seemed familiar, and now I remember. At the garden reception, one of the ladies mentioned that a housekeeper had been let go for stealing. Theft of a client's property, to be exact, but perhaps she was wrong. If Dora had accused the housekeeper of stealing bee hives, and the housekeeper had been fired because of that accusation, then—

"… and when I clap my hands twice …"

Recognizing the raspy, sibilant voice of Ransbleen Reiss, I pause in the hallway, trying to determine where his creepy voice is coming from.

" … you will open your eyes …"

Tiptoeing forward, glancing ahead at the four doors that lead into treatment rooms, I realize one of the doors is open. Quietly, crossing the hall, I take a quick look behind me, to make sure no one is around, and inch toward the door.

" ... and you will not recall what happened in this room ..."

Alarmed, I step closer, my pulse racing, wondering what could be happening.

" ... but before I do, I want to thank you very kindly for your donation to Save the Bees ..."

A gasp escapes my mouth before I can contain it, and almost immediately, I hear footsteps. Worried that Ransbleen might have heard me, I pivot, striding down the hall in the opposite direction, hoping I might be able to slip back into the relaxing room or—

"Ms. Cartier ... "

Wincing, I freeze, contemplating the idea of continuing to walk, pretending I didn't hear Ransbleen.

"Ms. Cartier ..."

Ransbleen's voice is closer behind me, and I realize I've waited too late to scurry away. Cursing my hesitation, I take a deep breath and face the general manager.

"Mr. Reiss," I say, plastering a fake smile on my face. "How are you?"

"I'm well, Ms. Cartier," says Ransbleen, giving me a ghoulish smile. "And I hope you don't find me impertinent if I say that you look well, also. Tell me, what treatment did you get?"

"The beeswax facial," I say, trying to discern if he suspects I was eavesdropping on whatever was happening in the room he was in. "It was great. My skin feels wonderful."

"I'm glad you enjoyed it and find the benefits satisfactory," he says. "Do you have another treatment scheduled?"

"Oh, no ..." I say. "Not today. I'm free for the rest of the afternoon."

"Well, I hope you enjoy it," says Ransbleen, his piercing gaze menacing.

Nodding, I tell him, "Thank you."

"Do you need an escort back to your room?"

Realizing that he wants me out of the treatment facility, I shake my head. "No, I can find my way back."

With a slight nod of his head, Ransbleen indicates that it's time for me to skedaddle, which I do, turning and hurrying down the long hallway. As I exit the building, I glance back. Ransbleen stands where I left him, staring at me …

Back in my room, I find Callie lounging on the bed.

I catch the cat up to speed on my sleuthing, informing her about the odd interaction with Ransbleen, and the strange things I'd overheard him say.

Licking her paw, the Calico says, "Reminds me of my friend Tabitha, she's a gray and white Tabby. Her owners thought she was too rambunctious, so they sent her to obedience training."

"Obedience training?" I echo, confused. "For a cat?"

"I know, right," agrees the cat. "Anyway, Tabby said they tried to trick her into being a well-behaved cat with all these crazy commands, and giving her catnip when she stopped hissing and scratching when they told her to. Of course, it didn't work."

"Crazy commands," I say, biting my lip. "I don't think Ransbleen was trying to do obedience training."

"Or, maybe he was," says the cat. "Obedience training is just training an animal to obey your command. Maybe Ransbleen is trying to train the clients to obey him when he tells them to donate money to the charity."

"Hmmm …" I say, considering it. "Or maybe—"

My cell phone goes off, signaling a text message.

"Who is it?" asks the cat.

Grabbing my phone, I access the message. "It's Officer Cuetee … he wants me to give him a call."

"Well, do it, girl," urges the cat. "He might have some information about the case."

I dial Officer Cuetee's number and wait for him to pick up.

"Sophie, where are you?" asks Officer Cuetee as soon as he answers.

"Oh, um … I'm at the Bee Well Medical Center," I say, pulling a face as I look at the cat, then whisper to her, "I forgot to tell Officer Cuetee where I am …"

"Well, you might as well tell him now," says the cat, licking her fur.

"The Bee Well Medical Center?" he asks, sounding confused. "What are you doing there?"

"Oh, um, you see …" I clear my throat as I walk toward the French doors leading out to the private terrace. "I'm on an undercover sting operation."

"An undercover sting operation?" asked Officer Cuetee, the confusion in his voice replaced by consternation.

"Yes, you see—"

"Sophie, why? You know things never work out when you go undercover," Officer Cuetee reminds me.

"That's true," I agree. "But, I'm thinking the third time is the charm."

Sighing audibly, Officer Cuetee asks, "So, exactly what are you doing on this sting?"

"I'm pretending to be a rich West Indian heiress who's at the medical center for its exclusive, world-renown bee product treatments," I say. "But, really, I'm looking for evidence to prove that Dora Butler was murdered."

"Have you found any proof, so far?"

"Not yet, but … " I began, then go on to inform Officer Cuetee of everything that's happened since I arrived.

He says, "Well, what I wanted to tell you is about Dora Butler's case."

"Have there been new developments?" I ask.

"You know how the CCTV showed Dora entering the day spa but not coming out?"

"Right," I say, recalling what he told me.

"Well, we discovered additional exterior video from another business across the street from the day spa," he says. "That video showed Dora leaving the day spa. She got into a car, which belonged to a woman named Marlo Green."

"That's her good friend," I say, remembering my conversation with the woman, who told the police she thought Dora had been murdered by an assistant beekeeper named Ida. Although, I realize now that can't possibly be true.

"Detective François spoke to Ms. Green, who said she drove Dora home," says Officer Cuetee. "Dora was very upset but didn't want to talk about why. The Ms. Green drove home."

"And then the next day, Dora Butler was found dead on the beach," I say.

"Which meant that Marlo Green might have been the last person to see Dora Butler alive before she was killed," says Officer Cuetee. "Which is why François checked out her story."

Shocked, I ask, "Detective François suspected Marlo Green?"

"He wanted to make sure she was telling the truth," says Officer Cuetee. "Turns out that she has several third-party apps on her phone used for GPS navigation that also track her location. She was telling the truth. Ms. Green picked up Dora and then drove to Dora's house. Ms. Green stayed there for about ten minutes."

"About long enough for Dora to get out of the car," I surmise.

"Exactly," says Officer Cuetee. "Then Ms. Green went home."

"And then someone killed Dora," I say. "And I think it was one of her coworkers here at the medical center."

"And you're determined to figure out who it was, right?"

Sensing resignation in his tone, I say, "I have to. Dora Butler deserves justice."

"Well, I can't stop you," says Officer Cuetee. "But please be careful Sophie. And if you get into any trouble, call me and let me know."

After my conversation with Officer Cuetee, Callie asks, "What did Officer Cuetee say?"

I relay the information to Callie, then say, "Which means that Dora was alive when Ransbleen left the day spa and got on the ferry the night they argued."

"He must have killed Dora when he came back," says the cat.

"I think he went to Bee Island to get the bee venom and dead bees," I say. "Then he returned to St. Mateo and killed Dora."

# Chapter 29

"Where is this … operating theater?" I ask Callie, following the cat down one of the many long, dark interconnected hallways of the treatment facility where spa procedures are done.

"This way, girl," says the cat, trotting along. "Follow me."

"Are you sure you know where you're going?" I ask, feeling more than a bit spooked as I glance around the treatment facility. As my footsteps echo on the polished floor, I can't help feeling that I'm being watched, maybe from the closed-circuit camera in a security room, and at any minute, a squad of guards will round the corner to round me up.

"I know exactly where I'm going," promises the cat.

I don't doubt her. My hesitation comes from the fact that, at night, when it's deserted, the treatment facility has a dark, sinister vibe. It's so different from the way it looked yesterday when I had the beeswax facial.

Thinking about yesterday, I'm reminded of Callie's theory concerning obedience training. I wasn't sure about it, but after ruminating about it a bit more, I wonder if she might be on to something, which I admit to her as we round yet another corner.

Callie says, "I think it makes sense."

"Yeah, but you can't trick someone into giving donations by giving them treats," I say.

Callie says, "Girl, I take it you've never enjoyed catnip."

Giggling, I say, "Can't say that I have."

"Good 'nip can definitely make you straighten up and fly right," says the cat.

"Possibly," I say. "But I don't think it could make someone give a large donation."

"Catnip, no," agrees the Calico. "But maybe ... what's the human equivalent to catnip?"

Shrugging, I glance over my shoulder again, afraid I'll see someone lurking behind me. "I don't know. Maybe alcohol. Or some type of narcotic."

"Let's blame it on the alcohol, as you humans love to do," says the cat. "Couldn't you give someone liquor to trick them into doing something?"

"I suppose you could," I say. "Liquor does lessen inhibitions and it can cause memory loss. But I don't think Ransbleen gave whoever he was talking to alcohol."

"Maybe he drugged them," suggests Callie.

"I'd be more inclined to believe that," I say, staying a few steps behind the cat. "But he said something about—"

"The operating theater is up ahead," announces Callie. "Last door on the right ..."

My heart races and my steps slow as I glance toward the door. I'm not looking forward to what's inside that room, considering what Callie told me yesterday as we ate dinner.

"So, I got the tea about this place from Benny the Rat," said Callie. "He's Sammy's second cousin."

"Sammy?"

"You know the rat who lives in the ladies' restroom at the *Palmchat Gazette.*"

I shuddered. "Don't remind me."

"Girl, it's either roaches or the rat," said the cat.

"What did Benny tell you?"

"Apparently, at the treatment facility, there's this operating theater," Callie said. "That's the place where Ransbleen Reiss makes the clients give donations."

"Does Benny know how he does that?"

"He's got no clue," informed the cat. "So you have to find out."

And that's what I'm about to do.

Standing in front of the door, I glance left, then right, down the hallway, making sure no one is coming. After all, it's after hours, and even though the facility is open until midnight, and it's a quarter past ten at night, I feel as though I'm sneaking around where I don't belong.

"Girl, what are you waiting for?" demands Callie. "Let's go inside."

"What if someone is in there?"

"Tell them you got lost," the cat says. "You were looking for the bathroom. You humans are always looking for the bathroom."

Nodding, I swallow my fear—some of it, not all—grab the knob, then wince as I twist it.

Inside, the room is about the size of a doctor's exam room, in the shape of a hexagon, with walls the color of honey. In the center of the room is what looks like a dentist's chair bolted to the floor. Above me, a honeycomb pattern crosses the ceiling and the floor is a swirling pattern of dark and light honey.

"Girl, what kind of room is this?" asks Callie, leaping onto the chair.

"I have no idea … " I say, turning in a slow circle as I look around. "But … it's sort of making me dizzy."

"Maybe that's the point, sis," says Callie, jumping to the floor. "Maybe you need to get dizzy enough to donate."

As I'm completing my revolution, I spot another door, directly across from the door Callie and I entered.

"Wonder what this opens to … " I step to the door, take a quick breath, grab the knob, and fling it open.

"What's inside?" asks Callie.

I peer into the dark recesses, wondering if I'll spot the entrance to an underground tunnel, or something equally intriguing but it seems to be a small, empty closet.

"Nothing," I say, turning from the door. "And other than this chair, there's nothing really in this room. Nothing that could prove that something nefarious is going on in here, or—"

"Uh-oh, sis … someone's coming," Callie says.

I glance down at the cat. "What? How do you know?"

"I can sense it," Callie insists. "And I can hear footsteps coming this way. Cats have excellent hearing."

"I know that, but—"

The knob on the door Callie and I entered starts to turn at the same time I hear muffled voices.

"Oh my gosh," I say, my heart thudding. "You were right."

"Girl, I know I'm right," Callie says. "What did I tell you? Cats know things. We gotta hide."

"The closet," I say, hurrying to the door I left halfway open. Callie and I scoot inside and I close the door until there's about an inch of an opening, enough for us to see.

"Come right this way …" says a raspy, reptilian voice.

"That's Ransbleen … " I whisper to Callie as the general manager enters the honey-colored room.

"Who is he talking to?" Callie whispers back.

"Can't see yet …" I say.

"Thank you kindly ..." says a jaunty, lyrical voice I know I've heard before.

"Please have a seat," says Ransbleen. "We'll get started shortly."

"I've been looking forward to this!"

Seconds later, I spot the other person in the room with Ransbleen.

"Oh my goodness ... "

"What?" demands Callie. "Girl, who is it?"

"Ethel Oliveria ..."

"Who?" demands the cat.

"One of the women I met at the garden reception," I whisper, apprehension sneaking through me as I wonder why Ethel is here. And what might happen to her?

"Before we start," says Ethel, settling herself onto the chair. "I want to thank you for allowing me to experience the secret serum."

"No need to thank me, the pleasure is mine," says Ransbleen. "I knew the moment I saw you that you would be a perfect candidate for this most exclusive procedure."

"What is he saying?" demands Callie.

"Something about an exclusive procedure," I say. "And a secret serum."

"I'm a perfect candidate because of all my wrinkles?" asks Ethel, a teasing note in her tone that seems to mask a hint of insecurity.

"On the contrary!" Ransbleen says. "A woman with too many wrinkles would not benefit from the secret serum. Only a woman with delicate skin who has previously known the dewy suppleness of youth will see results. You see, the secret serum is designed to facilitate the skin's memory so that the cells can recall their youthful appearance."

"He says Ethel's skin cells have to remember they're young, or something," I whisper to the cat.

"Girl, that sounds like goatwash."

I'm inclined to agree as Ransbleen continues to extol the benefits of the exclusive, secret serum. "This is the procedure that will make you look twenty years younger …"

"I doubt that," I snort.

"What?" asks Ethel.

"The procedure will make you look twenty years younger," repeats Ransbleen.

"No, I meant, what did you say after that?"

"I didn't say anything," says Ransbleen.

"Oh, I thought you did," says Ethel. "Perhaps I'm hearing things."

"Girl, what are they yapping about?" asks Callie.

Lowering my voice below a whisper, I say, "I think Ethel heard what I said about doubting that the procedure Ransbleen is going to give her will make her look twenty years younger."

"She needs to listen to you," says Callie.

"True, but I can't give our position away," I explain.

Ransbleen says, "Now, for the secret serum to be successful, I must speak to your skin cells."

"He's talking about speaking to her skin cells," I tell Callie.

"How is he supposed to do that?" The cat asks.

"I think he's going to tell her," I say.

"And in order to do this," says Ransbleen. "I must go deep into your consciousness, past your subconscious."

"And how will you do that?" asks Ethel.

I'm wondering the same thing, thinking it sounds … painful.

"Girl, what is he saying?"

"He's got to go into her subconscious to talk to her skin cells," I say, wishing Callie could remember how to understand humans. Unfortunately, due to her catnesia, she's lost that ability. Still, as much as I want her to regain it, I know if she does, she might remember who she really belongs to. If Callie recalls her real human, then I'll have to do the right thing and give her away. Life without the sassy, sarcastic talking cat fills me with dread, but I can't dwell on it.

Not when Ransbleen is explaining to Ethel how he plans to penetrate her subconscious.

"First, I will coat your face with a fine mist which will refresh the skin cells and encourage them to communicate with me," says Ransbleen.

Ethel giggles. "I wonder what my skin cells will say!"

"No doubt, they will insist you do not need this treatment," says Ransbleen, clearly buttering Ethel up.

"He's laying it on thick," I whisper to Callie.

"I'm guessing she's not seeing through it," says the cat.

"Unfortunately, no," I say, as Ransbleen sprays Ethel's face.

"Smells like honey," says the cat.

"I know," I say. "I wonder if it's the honey spray. Or, maybe … oh no …"

"What?" asks the cat.

An itchy tickle, or maybe a ticklish itch, spirals through my nose. "Whatever he sprayed is making me have to sneeze …"

"Girl, you can't sneeze," admonishes Callie. "He'll know we're hiding in here."

"I'll try not to … " I say, holding my nose. "But, I'm not sure I can … "

A whispery, squeaking ah-choo escapes, and immediately I wince when Ransbleen's head whips toward the closet. "Did you hear that?"

"Hear what?" asks Ethel, eyes closed as she relaxes in the chair. "Are you hearing things now?"

"Something in the closet …"

My heart rate spikes. "I think he heard me."

"Uh-oh, sis …" whispers Callie.

The Calico is right.

Ransbleen stomps toward the closet, his mouth set in a tight, grim line, eyebrows drawn together, framing the deep groove between them.

"Oh no," I whisper, frantic. "He's going to catch me … "

"Leave it to me, sis," says Callie. "Just get ready to run when I say run …"

"Okay," I say, taking a few steps back, hoping to hide in the back of the closet. "But what—"

A lively merengue tune fills the room.

"What …" Ransbleen pivots back to Ethel.

"Sorry, sorry …" apologizes Ethel. "My cell phone … it's my husband … I must take this call."

"Certainly," says Ransbleen. "We can continue the procedure at a later time. I'll escort you out."

With a curious glance toward the closet, Ransbleen takes Ethel by the elbow and leads her out of the hexagonal room, closing the door behind them.

Flooded with relief, I let out a long exhale. "That was close."

"Girl, let's get out of here before he remembers the noise he heard in the closet and comes back … "

"Yeah, good idea," I say, pushing the closet door open.

As Callie and I pass the reclining chair, I spot the can of spray. "Maybe I should take it."

Callie leaps onto the chair. "You could call Officer Cuetee so he can have it tested."

Glancing at the can, I rotate it, looking for an ingredient list, but there is none. It's just a honey-colored cylindrical can.

"You know," I say, removing the plastic top. "Maybe I could just—"

"What are you doing in here?"

# Chapter 30

"What am I doing in this room …" I sputter, glancing at Callie. "Oh, I was … um … "

"Girl, don't look at me," says the cat.

"You were … what?" demands the woman, a middle-aged, medium-height woman with brown hair pulled back in a ponytail. She's wearing the pale-yellow uniform of a Bee Well Medical Center housekeeper. As I stare at her dull, suspicious brown eyes, I can't help thinking she looks familiar.

Flustered, I say, "I was … "

"Lost, girl," says the cat, licking her paw. "Tell her you got lost. You know how directionally challenged you humans can be."

"I got … lost," I say.

"Why were you in this room?" demands the housekeeper, arms folded, gaze skeptical.

"I was looking for my cat," I say.

"Looking for your cat?" The Calico gives me a look. "What cat? Girl, you don't have a cat."

"Looking for your cat?" echoes the housekeeper, even though I know she didn't understand Callie.

"My cat was lost," I say, even though I know how independent Callie is and how much she hates it when I accidentally call her my cat. "And I saw her run into this building and I followed her … into this room … and thank goodness I found her, so … we'll just be leaving."

"Pretty good story, sis," says Callie, trotting toward the door. "Except for the part about me being lost. Cats have a very good sense of direction. That's why we always land on our feet."

"Have a good night," I say to the scowling housekeeper as I turn toward the door.

"Wait …" she commands.

"Yes?" I ask.

The housekeeper snatches the can of honey spray from my hand. "You won't be needing this."

Twenty minutes later, back in my suite, Callie and I are lounging on the bed, discussing how we avoided getting caught by Ransbleen but ended up being confronted by one of the housekeepers.

"You think she'll tell Ransbleen we were in the secret serum room?" I ask, staring at the ceiling.

"Who knows?" says the cat, licking her leg. "What I want to know is, why did she snatch that can out of your hand? Girl, you are better than me. The way I would have scratched her eyes right out of her head!"

Chuckling, I say, "Guess she had to spray it in someone's room. Which reminds me that I was thinking she seemed familiar to me. I think she's the same housekeeper I saw when we spotted the honey spray on the housekeeping cart. But, I'm not sure."

"What makes her seem familiar to you?" Callie asks.

"Strangely enough, her voice," I say. "Which doesn't make sense because she didn't say anything when I saw her in the bungalow. She was just cleaning."

"Okay, sis, enough about the housekeeper," says the cat. "What about the crypt keeper."

"What about him?"

"We were about to catch him in the act," says Callie. "Then Ethel got the phone call."

Sitting up, I say, "We'll have to try again. And I can try to record him so I'll have proof to give to Officer Cuetee."

"You think he was going to try to make Ethel obey?" asks Callie, licking her paw.

I tilt my head, thinking. "You know, I've been thinking about what I heard him say, when I first overheard him, after my beeswax facial, and … it sounded like … hypnosis."

"Hypnosis?" The cat stares at me.

Nodding, I say, "Ransbleen said he would clap his hands and then whoever he was talking to would wake up and not remember what happened in the room. Reminds me of a magic show I went to when I was in high school and our principal was hypnotized. The hypnotist said he would clap his hands twice and the principal would bleat like a goat. And then, he'd clap his hands once and the principal would come out of the hypnotic trance and not remember bleating like a goat."

"Girl, the crypt keeper doesn't want these clients to bleat like a goat."

"He wants them to give large donations to the Save the Bees charity," I say. "He might be hypnotizing the clients into giving him money. And maybe that's why they barely remember what happened at this place when they leave."

"But they do remember giving the donations," points out the cat.

"True, but I wonder if the hypnosis makes the clients not question their actions," I say. "The hypnotist gives the person a suggestion of something to do along with a command. Remember how Mrs. DuFault told me that she donates money when she gets a phone call and hears bees buzzing? So, the suggestion could be to donate money and the command is when you answer the phone and hear buzzing."

"Girl, you could be right," says Callie. "Hypnotizing is like obedience training. A command is given and you do it."

"Only, the cats and dogs know they're being trained," I say. "I don't think Ransbleen wants the clients to know they're being hypnotized. That's why he calls it a secret serum. He doesn't want them to tell anyone and he makes them feel special by claiming it's exclusive and they were hand-picked to receive it."

"Listen, sis, we need to figure out your next moves," says Callie, standing, then leaping off the bed. "But first, I need to use the little kitty's room. Let me out onto the patio and I'll be right back."

"I can come with you," I say, opening the French doors, worried about her trekking outside in the dark.

Callie gives me a look I know all too well.

"Okay, okay … but hurry."

I leave the doors open a crack, so the Calico can slip back inside, then walk to the wardrobe to get my pajamas. Pondering my next moves, I think getting a video of Ransbleen hypnotizing someone will be my best chance to prove he's using the power of suggestion to scam money from the medical center's rich clients.

Problem is, how can I find my way into the hexagonal room again?

I suppose Callie and I could make a return trip tomorrow night. Of course, we'd have to watch out for the housekeeper who confronted me, even though she doesn't know anything about Ransbleen's scam.

But, Ethyl might.

That is, Ethyl might help me get evidence against Ransbleen.

Not that I'm planning on asking her to sleuth with me.

Biting my lip, a plan forming in my mind, I grab the pajamas, turn, and—

A stream of aerosolized spray, fragrant with the cloying smell of honey, shoots toward my face.

Crying out in shock and fear, I close my eyes, coughing and sputtering. Completely blind, my heart slamming, I try to get my bearing, try to figure out what just happened to me, but I stumble forward, tripping, falling to the floor.

Gasping and hacking, trying to breathe, I glance up, trying to see, trying to make out the figure standing above me, but the hazy image starts to fade.

"Help ..." I rasp, my throat dry and itchy. "Please ... help ..."

The hazy silhouette comes closer as a deep dizziness overtakes me.

Quickly, steadily, darkness seeps in, shrouding me in nothingness

...

# Chapter 31

"Sis ... girl, wake up ..."

Something soft, furry, and sharp touches my cheek.

"Girl, don't go back into a coma ..."

Coma? I think, fighting the strange darkness swirling through my head. Why would I go back into a coma? Wait. Am I in a coma? No, I can't be in a coma. Not again. However, if I were, I probably wouldn't know it because I wouldn't be conscious which means I wouldn't be having any thoughts.

Although, some believe people in comas can hear—

"Sis, wake up!"

The soft, furry, sharp thing swats my chin.

"Ouch ..." I whisper, my eyelids fluttering as I carefully touch my skin where—

My eyes pop open and I sit upright, a little too fast because I feel sort of dizzy. Glancing ahead, I stare at Callie, who's standing on my legs, staring at me.

"You scratched me," I tell the Calico.

"Desperate times, desperate measures, as you humans would say," the Calico tells me. "I had to do something to wake you up."

"I was asleep?" I ask, glancing around my suite, focusing on my bed, which I'm not lying on. "Wait. Why am I on the floor?"

"Girl, you were out like a light!" Callie jumps off me. "After I did my evening business, I came back inside and you were sprawled on the floor."

"What?" I sigh, touching my temple, where a slight headache is forming. "Why was I sprawled on the floor?"

"I have no idea," says Callie, licking her paw. "I also have no idea why the housekeeper who confronted you was in your room going through your things."

"The housekeeper was going through my things?" I exclaim, scrambling to my feet. "Wait. What? Whoa …"

A lazy, sloshing feeling seeps through me, making me feel as though I'm going to pass out again, and I stumble, trying to keep my balance.

"Careful, sis," says Callie, leaping onto the bed. "You look like you had too much catnip. Come over here and lie down."

Taking the cat's advice, I plop down onto the bed, swing my legs up over the side, and sink back into the pillows propped against the headboard.

"Girl, I think that housekeeper hit you in the head," says Callie, settling into a loaf next to me.

Clearing my throat, I feel a strange, itchy tickle and the residual taste of something medicinal with a hint of honey. At once, a memory invades my mind. "No, that's not what happened. I was getting my pajamas and then I turned around and someone sprayed something in my face."

"What was it?"

"I think it might have been that honey spray she snatched from me when we were leaving," I say. "But why would she do that?"

"So she could go through your things," says Callie. "She was all in your purse when I came in."

"Why would she go through my purse?" I ask, glancing at the dresser where I keep my purse in the top drawer … which is open. In fact, several of the drawers are open. "What was she looking for?"

"You need to make sure nothing is missing," says Callie. "But first, you need to call your PSA so she can report this to security."

Nodding, I rise again and reach for the suite phone on the bedside table. "You're right."

Fifteen minutes later, my PSA, Suzie, is sitting on the bed next to me, her expression worried and wary as she assures me that she plans to inform security about what happened to me.

"I'm so sorry you experienced this," says Suzie. "It's so terrible."

"Is she going to call the cops?" asks Callie.

"You're going to talk to security, right?" I ask, not for confirmation, but as an answer to Callie, in a way that won't alert Suzie to the fact that I can understand the Calico.

Suzie nods. "Yes, dear. And they'll want to interview you, but not tonight. I'll send a nurse over to make sure you're okay. You can speak with security in the morning."

"Thank you, I appreciate that."

"Security will make the rounds around your suite tonight," says Suzie.

"That will make me feel much better," I say.

"What will make you feel better?" demands Callie.

"The idea of security making sure my room is secure is reassuring," I say, for the cat's benefit.

"Girl, security doesn't need to secure your room," says Callie. "They need to arrest that crazy honey-spraying housekeeper."

Shaking my head, I say, "Security doesn't have jurisdiction."

Suzie frowns. "I'm sorry?"

"Oh, um …" Once again, I could kick myself for forgetting not to talk to the cat while I'm talking to other people. "I was thinking out loud … your security guards don't have jurisdiction to arrest anyone."

"No, but they are deputized to apprehend suspects and hold them until the police show up," says Suzie. "So, if anyone is lurking around your room tonight, that's what they'll do."

"Good to know," I tell Suzie, as she stands to leave. "And again, thank you so much."

"I know it might be hard, but try to relax," says Suzie. "The nurse will be here soon."

After Suzie leaves, Callie asks, "Girl, why didn't you tell her that the housekeeper attacked you?"

"I'm going to talk to security tomorrow," I tell the cat. "I didn't want to tell Suzie because, although I like her, coworkers gossip. I don't want the housekeeper to know I'm on to her. She might come up with a story to refute my version of events."

"Girl, you mean my version of events," corrects the cat. "I'm the one who caught her going through your purse and stopped her."

"What did you do?" I ask, crossing the room to the dresser. "Scratch her eyes out?"

"She's lucky I didn't," says the cat, licking her leg. "Instead, I hissed at her and scratched her hands. She got out of here quick."

Grabbing my purse, I take it to the sitting area, sink down onto the plush divan, and look inside.

"Anything missing?" Callie leaps up onto the divan.

"Unfortunately, something very important is missing," I say, fishing through the things in my purse, hoping I overlooked what I'm afraid the housekeeper took. "My press pass … "

# Chapter 32

"I thought I would be speaking with the head of security," I say, apprehension coursing through me as I glance warily at the man sitting behind the desk.

Ransbleen Reiss gives me his customary ghoulish smile. "Ms. Cartier, as the general manager, I also oversee all aspects of security."

"Oh ..." I say, disquieted by the information. "Well ..."

Last night, after seeing the nurse, who helped me flush my eyes and gave me a mild sedative I went to bed, restless and worried. Callie slept at my feet, and when I woke up this morning, we had breakfast and engaged in a bit of speculation about last night's events.

Basically, the questions are ...

What did the housekeeper spray me with? Was it the honey spray? If so, why? Does she know about the memory loss it causes? If so, did she use it so I would forget the attack? And what was she looking for in my purse? Is she a thief? Did she steal my press pass? If so, why? And now that she knows who I really am, what does she plan to do with the information? Will she tell Dr. Napier? Will he demand to know why I'm at the center under a fake name? Will he assume I'm trying to do an exposé on the medical center? Or, recognizing that I'm the reporter who covered Dora Butler's murder, will he think I'm undercover to find clues about her death? Of course, Dr. Napier would only think that if he knew there was something shady and nefarious about the way Dora died. He would only suspect that if he's aware that Dora was murdered …

Callie thinks the housekeeper was suspicious of me because she caught me snooping in the hexagon room, a place I shouldn't have been. Maybe she wanted to figure out what I was up to, which is possible. It's also a problem because if she took my press pass, then—

"Ms. Cartier …" prompts Ransbleen. "Tell me what happened."

The last person I expected to talk to about the attack was Ransbleen Reiss. After breakfast, Suzie, my PSA stopped by to check on me and inform me that security wanted to meet with me about the attack last night. Callie opted to stay in bed to sleep a bit longer. When Suzie took me to the administration building, led me through a series of hallways, and ended at the office of Ransbleen Reiss, I was shocked and disappointed.

But, now I'm thinking I might be able to find out if the housekeeper told him who I really am, and how she caught me in the hexagonal room with the can of honey spray.

"Suzie said you were attacked in your room?" Ransbleen leans back in his chair, staring at me. "Tell me everything that happened."

"Okay, well …" I clear my throat, looking away from his baleful stare, glancing around his spacious office, which reminds me of a terrarium, with its glass walls surrounded by lush vegetation. "I don't remember very much."

"What exactly do you remember?" he asks, his gaze suspicious.

"I was getting ready for bed," I say. "I went to the wardrobe and got my pajamas. Then when I turned, someone sprayed something in my face. It blinded me for a few seconds and then everything went black."

"Everything went black ..." repeats Ransbleen, his gaze skeptical.

"I collapsed," I tell him. "I'm not sure how long I was unconscious."

"Those details were in Nurse Clare's report," says Ransbleen, glancing at a document on his desk. "However, she was unable to determine any foreign substances on your skin, suggesting that you might have been drugged."

"The spray smelled like ... " I take a deep breath before saying, "... honey."

Ransbleen lifts his head. "Ms. Cartier, this is the Bee Well Medical Center. Everything here smells like honey."

"Yes, well," I say. "It was some type of honey spray."

"Honey spray?"

Nodding, I say, "And I think I know who did it."

With his elbows on the surface of the desk, Ransbleen steeples his fingers. "You know the attacker?"

"Well, I don't know her," I say. "I mean, I don't know her name. I've never met her."

"Her?"

"One of the housekeepers."

"You believe one of the housekeepers sprayed you with a foreign substance that smelled like honey?" asks Ransbleen, leaning back again.

"I'm sure of it," I say.

"Why do you think that?"

"Well, because ..." I trail off, suddenly aware of my conundrum. I can't tell Ransbleen that I know the housekeeper attacked me because Callie, the talking cat who talks to me, saw her. I also can't let him know that I saw the housekeeper myself in the hexagonal room, because I wasn't supposed to be there.

"Because?"

Clearing my throat, I say, "Because … I saw her."

"And what did she look like?"

Recalling the housekeeper, I say, "She was … "

"And when did you see the housekeeper spray you?" asks Ransbleen.

"When did I see her?"

"Well, you said that you were sprayed and everything went black," he says, giving me a malicious smirk. "If you were unconscious, then when did you see the housekeeper?"

Kicking myself for the mistake, I say, "I must have gotten a quick glimpse of her before she sprayed me."

"I see …" remarks Ransbleen, his tone doubtful.

"Do you know her name?" I ask, ignoring his suspicion of me. "The housekeeper I described to you."

"I'm afraid I don't recall a housekeeper fitting that description," says Ransbleen. "And I am in charge of hiring all staff. However, she may be a new hire, and perhaps I haven't memorized her face."

"Well, are you going to check your HR files?" I ask. "I think the housekeeper should be arrested. She attacked me and went through my purse."

"Ms. Cartier, I am taking this matter very seriously," insists Ransbleen. "And I plan to conduct a thorough investigation, and—"

The phone on Ransbleen's desk rings, a jarring sound that makes me jump.

Frowning, Ransbleen says, "Excuse me one moment …"

As Ransbleen answers the phone, I glance around his office, so I won't appear to be listening to his conversation. There's not much furniture other than his desk, and the chairs in front of his desk, one of which I'm sitting in. My initial assessment of his office as a terrarium has to be modified as there are only two glass walls, one to my left, and the other to my right. Behind Ransbleen is a solid wall, where two narrow bookcases flank an empty space that's about as wide as a door. It looks like a place for a nice piece of artwork, but Ransbleen doesn't seem the type to appreciate art, or—

"Yes … what?" Ransbleen whispers, his frown deepening. "No, no … don't do anything, just stay where you are, I'll be right there."

After replacing the phone receiver onto the base, Ransbleen looks at me. "Ms. Cartier, I'm afraid there's something I need to attend to …"

"Everything okay?" I ask, as he seems flustered and distracted.

"It will be," he says, standing. "I regret we have to cut our meeting short, but security has been informed of the incident which occurred in your suite and they have been ordered to make regular patrols, however, I believe what happened to you was an isolated event. You have no need to worry. You are safe here."

"Well, thank you …" I stand, then walk to the door, and open it. Stepping out into the hallway, I grab the handle to close the door and notice Ransbleen standing at the bookshelf on the left, his back to me. He grabs a book from the shelf and then steps into the space between the bookshelves.

Confusion, and curiosity, overtake me, pushing aside the apprehension, and the worry that someone will catch me.

The space between the bookshelves opens.

I stifle a gasp as Ransbleen exits the office, hurrying out into the lush jungle.

# Chapter 33

"How are we going to get back into the crypt keeper's office?" asks Callie, trotting beside me as we make our way through the hallways of the administration building, staying close to the walls, mindful of our surroundings, careful not to cause any unwanted attention from the various medical center staff we encounter.

Fifteen minutes have passed since I saw Ransbleen exit his office through a secret passageway between the bookshelves on the back wall. Now I realize why the space between the shelves is blank. A painting on the wall would block his access to the secret door.

After Ransbleen disappeared, I hurried back to my room to debrief Callie.

The Calico agreed that we needed to go back to Ransbleen's office and find out where the pathway leads.

"When I left his office," I say, turning yet another corner. "I didn't close the door all the way. I left a really small crack, so hopefully, we'll be able to get back in."

"What if the crypt keeper is back in his office?" asks the cat.

"There is that possibility," I acknowledge. "I'll tell him I thought I left something in his office. Like, my phone, or something."

"And if he's not in his office, how do we access the secret door to the outside?" asks Callie. "I'm assuming he closed it behind him when he left."

"You're right about that," I say, making a right turn down the corridor leading to Ransbleen's office, at the end of the hall. "But, I think I know how he made the door open."

As Callie and I approach the door to Ransbleen's office, my heart pounds. I'm hoping the door is still opened slightly, the way I left it. If it's not, it might mean one of two things. Perhaps some staff member noticed the door was open and closed it. Or, Ransbleen is back in his office.

A few moments later, steps away from the door, Callie trots ahead.

"Is there a crack in the door?" I whisper, glancing over my shoulder.

"See for yourself … " advises the cat as she stretches up, locks her paws around the doorknob, then pushes her body forward, swinging the door open.

"Callie … " I say, rushing behind her, praying Ransbleen isn't sitting behind his desk, giving me a ghoulish smile, waiting to tell me that he knows exactly who I am and exactly why I'm here.

But the office is empty.

Dim and frosty from the A/C.

"Okay, sis, let's find out where the secret door leads," says Callie, leaping onto the chair I was sitting on earlier.

Breathing a sigh of relief, I hurry to close the door, then turn to face the Calico, now perched on Ransbleen's desk. "Okay, I saw him take a book off the shelf and then the secret door opened."

"Which book? Which shelf?" asks the cat.

Scurrying behind the desk, I struggle to remember. The right bookshelf? Or the left? And which shelf? Each bookcase has six shelves. I seem to remember Ransbleen pulling a book from the middle shelf. Maybe the third. As for which book, I'm not sure.

Biting my lip, I grab a book from the third shelf on the right bookcase. "Here goes nothing …"

A few seconds pass, but the secret door doesn't open.

"And nothing happened," says Callie. "Think, sis. Was the book toward the left end of the shelf, or the right end."

Closing my eyes, I try to envision the moment when I saw Ransbleen access the secret door. I think he was standing in front of the left bookcase. And he chose a book close to him.

"Let me try … this one …" I say, pulling a copy of Roget's Thesaurus from the bookshelf.

Seconds pass.

My heart slams.

Nothing happens.

Licking her leg, Callie says, "Try again, sis."

Blowing out a breath of frustration, I grab the next book, a guide to Caribbean flora and fauna.

Seconds pass.

My heart slams.

Nothing happens.

Licking her paw, Callie says, "Try again, sis. And hurry it up. We don't have all day."

I give the cat a look.

Then I try the next book, a medical dictionary. When nothing happens, I try the next book, a field guide. It doesn't work, so I try an encyclopedia of coffee beans. Then I try a copy of—

"Girl, it worked!" announces Callie.

"What?" I glance at the cat as a humid breeze wafts toward me.

I look straight ahead.

The wall between the bookshelves is gone!

# Chapter 34

"Oh my gosh," I say, staring down the narrow dirt path through thick jungle vegetation. "Wait. Which book was the right one?"

"Girl, who cares," says the Calico, jumping down from the desk and heading onto the path. "Let's see where this leads."

Pushing aside my worries, I cross the threshold from Ransbleen's office onto the dirt path. Callie trots ahead of me. I take a few cautious steps, breathing in the scent of sea air and hibiscus. A faint swishing sound, behind me, makes me jump and I look over my shoulder.

The opening to Ransbleen's office is closed.

Turning, I face what looks like a stucco wall, my heart pounding, wondering how Callie and I will get back into the medical center. Surrounded by trees, I suddenly feel trapped, even though I'm outside and could probably find my way back to my room. After all, if I stand still, I can hear the ocean. I shake off the willies I'm suddenly feeling. It's not like I've never been in the jungle before, surrounded by clusters of trees and bushes and shrubs.

"Girl, come on!" demands the cat.

"Coming, coming …" I say, following her along the path, pushing past giant, waxy dark green elephant leaves as we meander through the bushes and shrubs. The questions in my head center around the reason for this path. Why would Ransbleen have a secret door leading out to the jungle? Where does the path lead? What will Callie and I find at the end of it? Assuming there is an end and it doesn't just lead to the beach.

A giggle escapes me.

"Girl, what are you laughing about?" asks Callie, stopping to stare up at me.

Shaking my head, I say, "I was thinking this could be a path to nowhere. Just a way for Ransbleen to get to the beach."

"I don't think so," says Callie. "You said he was talking to someone about staying where they were and he would be right there."

"Yeah, that's right," I say, recalling the call that interrupted our meeting. "He sounded upset and frustrated. Like maybe something was going wrong."

"He was heading somewhere specific," says Callie, taking off down the path.

"Wait up ..." I tell her, carefully navigating the trail as it descends at a slight slope that's sharp enough for me to lose my footing if I'm not careful.

Reflecting on my interrupted meeting with Ransbleen, though he seemed doubtful about my attack, I'm not sure he didn't believe me. It was more like he did believe me but didn't want me to make too much of what happened, despite his insistence that he planned to do a full investigation.

Slipping through a section of oleander bushes and banana trees, I follow the trail as it veers sharply to the left.

I also don't believe that Ransbleen doesn't know the housekeeper I described to him. He's the general manager of the medical center. He runs the entire place and nothing gets past him. So, if he knows the housekeeper, why would he pretend not to? Could he be covering for her? Maybe not wanting her to get in trouble for attacking me? Or, could it be possible that Ransbleen sent the housekeeper to drug me, then snoop through my room?

I suppose, if the housekeeper told Ransbleen she saw me in the hexagonal room, he could have gotten suspicious and then ordered the housekeeper to investigate me. Although, considering that he gives directions to security, why didn't he have one of the guards go through my room when I was having a procedure?

I'm not sure, but—

"Girl, come on," says Callie, scampering toward me. "There's a shack at the end of the trail and the crypt keeper is in there."

Hurrying after the Calico, I continue down the path through the trees, following it right, then left, then right again until Callie stops near a cluster of bushes. Hiding behind the thick leaves, I peek through the branches. Tucked into a small clearing surrounded by palm trees, the shack is nothing more than three walls constructed of weather-beaten driftwood with a rusted corrugated roof on top.

The interior is dim, but I can make out Ransbleen … and the person with him.

"Ransbleen is with the housekeeper who attacked me … " I whisper to Callie as excitement and apprehension races through me. Excitement because this is a huge lead, one that can help me prove that Ransbleen is doing something shady and criminal. But I'm apprehensive because I'm sure, now more than ever, that Ransbleen is dangerous. He obviously knows the housekeeper. He might not have sent her to attack me, but I'm sure she told him I was in the hexagonal room, and if she took my press pass, which I'm sure she did, then she told Ransbleen my real name.

"What are they saying?" Callie asks.

"Let me get a bit closer," I say, venturing around the bushes, stepping lightly, and then scurrying to one of the side walls, where I'm out of sight, but able to hear Ransbleen and the housekeeper.

"… you'll get your cut of the money at the end of the week … " says Ransbleen.

"I need the money right now," insists the housekeeper. "I need to get off this island."

"That's not my problem."

"It might not be your problem," says the housekeeper. "But it is your fault!"

"Don't blame me for your stupid decision," warns Ransbleen.

"My *stupid decision,* as you call it," says the housekeeper, "kept you out of jail!"

"You're giving yourself way too much credit," says Ransbleen. "And you're not giving me what I need, which is more of that honey spray."

"I'm not making any more of that hypno-spray until I get my money," says the housekeeper.

"You better get me more of that spray," says Ransbleen. "Or … you'll end up like Dora Butler."

"Are you threatening me?" demands the housekeeper.

Callie trots toward me, slinking her body between my ankles. Lifting my right foot, I glance down at her. "What are you doing?" I whisper.

"Don't scream, sis," says the cat, crouching low. "But there's a mouse."

"A mouse …" I stifle a gasp, then lift my left foot as the cat leaps along the side of the shack, pouncing on something small and furry. Trying not to shriek, I sidestep to the left, away from Callie, and my foot lands on a fallen branch, snapping it in half.

"What was that noise?" demands Ransbleen.

"What noise?" asks the housekeeper. "I didn't hear anything."

"Shut up …" Ransbleen tells her.

"What's going on, sis?" whispers Callie, her paw firmly on the neck of the field mouse.

"We gotta hide," I tell the Calico, hurrying away from the shack into a bramble of oleander bushes. Callie follows, scurrying beneath the undergrowth. Positioning myself behind the branches, I push the leaves aside. Ransbleen walks around the side of the shack, examining the area where Callie and I were just standing.

As I hold my breath, willing myself not to move, wary of accidentally rustling branches and calling attention to myself, Ransbleen continues to look around. His expression grim and ghastly, he peers intently at the trees, and for a moment, I wonder if he can see me.

"What did you hear?" asks the housekeeper, joining him.

"Maybe it was a rat or something," says Ransbleen, frowning. "Come on, let's get back to the center."

# Chapter 35

"Girl, that was close!" says Callie, jumping up onto the bed as I close the door to my suite.

Breathing yet another sigh of relief, I join her, belly-flopping onto the soft mattress. "Way too close!"

After Ransbleen and the housekeeper left the shack, heading along the dirt path back to his office, Callie and I took another route, guided by Callie's keen sense of smell, which led to the beach, where we took a long, meandering, but relatively pleasant walk back to the medical center.

"Well, at least you know the crypt keeper and the housekeeper are working together," says the cat. As we walked, I told her what I overheard.

"True," I say, flipping onto my back. "The housekeeper is making the honey spray and Ransbleen is paying her for it. He's using the spray to hypnotize clients into giving large donations to the Save the Bees charity."

"Girl, they're probably writing checks that he deposits into his bank account," says the cat, licking her paw.

"That's what I need to do," I say, sitting up.

"What's what you need to do?" asks Callie, staring at me.

"Follow the money," I say. "I need to write Ransbleen a check."

"Girl, don't forget that you're not rich," says the cat. "Sophia Cartier doesn't exist."

"But, Ransbleen doesn't know that," I say. "Well, not unless the housekeeper told him, which she might have."

"If he knows who you really are," says Callie, "don't you think he would kick you out of this place?"

"Maybe ..."

"Think about it, sis," says the cat. "If the housekeeper took your press pass and told the crypt keeper you're a reporter, and that you were sneaking around in the room where he does the hypnosis, then he would assume you're investigating him. And he wouldn't want you anywhere near this place. He'd come up with some reason for why you need to leave. Why would he let you stay here?"

"Maybe he wants to get rid of me like he got rid of Dora Butler," I suggest.

"Girl, please," says the cat. "If that was true, he would have had you killed when you were unconscious."

"I suppose you're right," I say.

"I wouldn't have let it happen, though," says Callie.

"That's so sweet of you," I tell the cat, reaching to scratch her head, which she, surprisingly, allows me to do.

"I would have scratched her eyes right out of her head," insists the Calico.

"I would have expected nothing less," I say, smiling at her. "But, let's assume Ransbleen doesn't know I work for the *Palmchat Gazette*. If the housekeeper didn't tell him—because maybe she wants to keep that information to herself for some reason since it seems they don't trust each other—then, he still believes I'm a rich heiress. And as a rich heiress, I can donate to his charity."

"Girl, with what money?"

"Well," I begin, "Leo and Vivian approved the funding of this sting operation. I'm sure I can convince them to appropriate additional funds so I can follow the money, which I am sure will lead me to some off-shore account controlled by Ransbleen."

"And what if they don't?" asks the cat.

"Maybe I can ask my friend Stevie," I say. "He works at the *Palmchat Gazette* in St. Killian. And he's the son of the billionaire family that owns Felipe Beer."

"So, your friend Stevie is rich *rich*," says the cat, licking her paw.

Laughing, I say, "If he was a feline, you'd call him an *aristocat*."

"Okay, sis," says Callie. "Sounds like a good plan. But, you can't get yourself hypnotized. The last thing you want is to forget everything you find out."

"Right," I agree. "Which is why I plan to tell Ransbleen that I want to donate to the charity because I love bees and I'm concerned about their possible extinction because they're so important to our ecosystem. But, I won't need the secret serum because, well ... I'm twenty-three and I don't have wrinkles."

"Girl, you and me both," says Callie. "People always mistake me for a kitten!"

# Chapter 36

"What did Vivian and Leo say about your idea to follow the money?" asks Callie, lounging on the bistro table where I'm sitting, enjoying the early morning sunshine and cool sea breezes.

At seven in the morning, the garden café is all but empty. There are only two other clients, a duo of octogenarians several tables away, having juice and pastries. As such, I'm okay with talking to the talking cat, but I still keep my voice low and try to keep my hand in front of my mouth as I speak. I don't need to be caught openly conversing with a feline.

"They're on board with it," I say, taking a bite of the guava, papaya, and pineapple fruit salad I'm having for breakfast. Yesterday evening, I had a long conversation with the publisher and my mentor, outlining the results of the sting so far, and explaining my idea to expose Ransbleen's charity scheme.

"Vivian did some quick research," I say, wishing I had tea and donut holes even though the fruit is nice and fresh, and healthier. "And as I suspected, the Save the Bees charity doesn't even exist. And yet people are donating to it."

"That's fraud," says Callie.

"That's what Vivian and Leo think I might be able to prove," I say, thrilled by my bosses' endorsement and encouragement. "And I'm sure that's what Dora Butler found out. That Ransbleen and the housekeeper developed a hypnotic honey spray to trick clients into donating to their fake charity."

"A definite motive for murder," says the cat.

"I'm not sure how to prove that Ransbleen killed Dora—yet," I say. "But with proof that he's scamming clients and Dora's diary, I can write a story that I'm sure will compel Detective François to reopen Dora's case."

"You need that detective to investigate Ransbleen and the housekeeper," says Callie. "You still need to get a can of that spray so Officer Cuetee can have it tested."

Nodding, I say, "That's also on my to-do list—"

"Well, you better do something about it!" shouts an angry male voice, causing me to look up. The beekeeper, Dr. Jones, and the founder of the medical center, Dr. Napier, walk into the garden center. The beekeeper looks even more disheveled while Dr. Napier looks disappointed and frustrated.

"Girl, what's his problem?" asks the cat. "What is he yelling about?"

"I'm not sure," I say. "The beekeeper wants Dr. Napier to do something about something, but I'm not sure what ..."

"Will you please calm down?" asks Dr. Napier, waddling behind the beekeeper.

"This is unacceptable!" says the beekeeper, yanking a chair from beneath a bistro table near a wall of oleander bushes. "Fix it or I will quit!"

"Please, don't be rash," cautions Dr. Napier, glancing around the garden café, focusing on the octogenarians, and then staring at me.

Quickly, I look down and shove a chunk of pineapple in my mouth.

"Are they arguing?" asks Callie.

I glance at the cat. "The beekeeper threatened to quit."

"Why?" Callie asks.

"I don't know," I say, surreptitiously glancing over my shoulder. The beekeeper and Dr. Napier are sitting at the table, their voices lowered as they continue what appears to be a heated discussion.

"Well, you need to find out," says the cat, licking her hind leg.

"Well, I'm trying but I don't have your superior hearing," I say.

"Sucks not to be a cat, doesn't it?" asks the feisty feline.

I open my mouth to give her a sassy retort when I feel something bump my shoulder.

Gasping, I look up.

"Sorry ..." mumbles the beekeeper. "I need to watch where I'm going. Please excuse me ..."

"Oh, no, it's fine," I say, then jump up to follow him as he walks away. "Dr. Jones ... Dr. Jones."

Facing me, the beekeeper scowls, squinting in the bright sunlight. "Yes?"

"I wanted to tell you that I think the bee products at the center are outstanding," I say, trying to think of how I might be able to get the tea about his argument with Dr. Napier. "And—"

"Just be thankful you were able to experience the products," grumbles the beekeeper. "You might have had your one and only chance."

"What do you mean?" I ask.

"Three bee hives were stolen yesterday," grouses the beekeeper.

"What? How?" I ask, shocked. "Do you know why? Or have any idea who would have done something so awful?"

Dr. Jones frowns, then says, "I wish I knew. Dora did ..."

"Dora Butler?" I say, my interest ignited. "I was told she passed away."

Shaking his head, the beekeeper says, "Last time I spoke to her,

Dora told me she had proof that one of the housekeepers was stealing the bee hives.

"One of the housekeepers," I repeat, thinking of the woman who caught me in the hexagonal room, and then later attacked me.

"Unfortunately, Dora didn't get to tell me who it was," says the beekeeper. "She came up dead before she had the chance."

# Chapter 37

"Oh, Dr. Napier," I say. "Hello …"

"How are you doing, Ms. Cartier?" asks the medical center founder, standing outside the door to my suite.

After my conversation with the beekeeper, Callie and I returned to my room and engaged in speculation about the missing bee hives. The cat and I are more convinced than ever that the housekeeper who attacked me probably stole the hives, considering I overheard Ransbleen telling her to make more of the hypnotic honey spray. She must need the beeswax, pollen, and honey to create the diabolical concoction.

"I'm fine," I tell the medical director. "How are you?"

"Well, at the moment," says Dr. Napier. "I am more concerned about you. Would you mind terribly if we spoke for a moment?"

"No, not at all," I say, stepping back to allow him entry. "Come in …"

"Girl, what does he want?" asks Callie, hissing at the doctor.

"I'm not sure," I mumble.

"I'm sorry?" asks the doctor, smiling at Callie, walking toward her. "What a lovely cat. Hi pretty girl."

"Girl, you better tell him not to touch me," warns Callie, arching her back.

"My cat is a little cranky today," I tell the doctor as I pick Callie up and place her on the floor next to my feet. "Sorry ..."

"No, it's fine," says the doctor, as he faces me, then gives me a smile that doesn't reach his eyes. "I'm more concerned with you. Your PSA Suzie told me about the unfortunate event that occurred in your suite."

"I was attacked by one of the housekeepers," I tell him, leading him to the sitting area. "She sprayed me with some sort of honey-smelling substance."

"Yes, Ransbleen informed me," says the doctor, taking a seat on one of the divans. "And your nurse gave you a clean bill of health."

"But, I was still attacked, Dr. Napier," I say. "I believe the police should be notified."

"I hope it doesn't have to come to that," says Dr. Napier. "Perhaps if I comped your stay? And threw in a few more facial procedures?"

"Well ..." I say, as an idea occurs to me. "I wouldn't mind experiencing the secret serum procedure."

Dr. Napier frowns. "Secret serum? I'm afraid I don't know what you mean."

"Felice DuFault, who recommended this place to me, told me she got a special secret serum," I say, not exactly shocked that Dr. Napier seems unaware of Ransbleen's hypnosis scam. "She says it works by encouraging your aging skin cells to rejuvenate themselves."

Dr. Napier chuckles. "If only it was that easy. I'm not sure what Mrs. DuFault was referring to, but we don't have any procedures like that here. Maybe she meant another facility."

"Possibly," I say.

"Is there any other procedure you're interested in?" asks the doctor, obviously eager to convince me not to go to the police and bring unwanted attention and scrutiny to the facility.

"What I'm truly interested in is making sure I'm not attacked again," I say. "I spoke with Mr. Reiss about the matter but he didn't take it seriously. He claimed the housekeeper I described didn't sound like anyone who works here."

"What did she look like?" asks Dr. Napier.

I describe the housekeeper, then ask, "Does she seem familiar to you?"

The doctor scowls. "I'm not surprised Reiss wasn't honest with you."

"What do you mean?"

"The housekeeper you described is Reiss's cousin," says Dr. Napier. "She's obviously up to her old tricks. I never should have let him convince me to rehire her. She hasn't changed. She was accused of theft, and while the allegations were never proven, I suspect they were true."

"Do you think she had anything to do with the stolen hives?" I ask.

Dr. Napier's eyes narrow. "You know about that?"

"I spoke with Dr. Jones," I say. "He suspected a housekeeper had stolen the hives, but he couldn't remember her name."

"I wouldn't be surprised if Marlo stole the bee hives," says Dr. Napier. "I swear that woman is a kleptomaniac."

Something Dr. Napier said sets off an alarm in me. "Wait a minute. What is the housekeeper's name?"

His face twisted with disgust, Dr. Napier says, "Marlo Green."

# Chapter 38

"Who is Marlo Green?" asks Callie, lying on the bed, staring at me as I pace around my suite.

"Marlo Green is Ransbleen Reiss's cousin," I say. "She's the housekeeper who attacked me. And more than that, she's a good friend of Dora Butler. I actually talked to her about Dora's murder."

"What did she say?" asks Callie. "Did you already tell me?"

"I'm not sure," I say. "But, Marlo was the one who first told me that Dora had been investigating shady business at the medical center and that she thought Dora had been murdered."

"And come to find out, she's a thieving housekeeper whipping up toxic spray that her cousin uses to hypnotize rich women so they'll make donations to his fake charity," summarizes the cat.

"That's why her voice sounded so familiar," I say.

"Girl, she probably recognized you, too," says Callie.

"Maybe that's why she attacked me," I say. "She realized who I was, and might have suspected I was undercover, trying to find out what happened to Dora."

"Wonder why she took your press pass," says the cat.

Shrugging, I say, "Who knows? I wonder why she didn't tell me that she worked with Dora at the medical center. And why would she tell me that Dora knew about shady business going on here considering she's involved in the shady business Dora found out about."

"Maybe she got scared when Dora was murdered," suggests the cat.

Nodding, I say, "Dora might have confronted Marlo about stealing bee hives. And then Marlo told her cousin Ransbleen that Dora was on to their scheme. And then … Ransbleen killed Dora. That probably scared Marlo, who never thought her cousin would actually kill Dora."

"Marlo might have snitched on her cousin to save her own life."

"I did overhear Ransbleen threatening Marlo," I say. "He told her he wanted her to make more of the hypnotic spray or she'd end up like Dora."

The cat says, "Okay, so, we know that Dora Butler found out about Ransbleen's scam."

"And he killed her because she was going to expose them."

"Girl, you've solved the case," says Callie.

"But I still have to prove Ransbleen is a murderer," I say. "I'm still going to tell him I want to donate to the Save the Bees charity, which will help me prove the financial scam. But I need proof that he injected Dora with bee venom."

"Maybe you can convince Marlo to come clean to the cops," suggests Callie. "She told them she thought Dora was murdered. Now she needs to give them a suspect—her cousin."

"He has a motive. He has means—access to bee venom," I say. "And he had plenty of opportunity."

"Don't forget, he argued with Dora the night she died," the cat reminds me. "Then they drove to the medical spa. And Dora never came out …"

"Actually, Dora did come out of the day spa, remember?" I tell the cat. "Officer Cuetee told me that Marlo Green picked up Dora and drove her home."

Bobbing her head, Callie says, "And then the crypt keeper probably went back to Dora's house and killed her."

"I'll bet he went to Bee Island, got the venom, then …" I trail off as a memory distracts me.

"Then came back to St. Mateo and injected Dora," finishes the Calico.

Frowning, I walk to the bed and sit down. "Maybe …"

The cat gives me a look. "Girl, what do you mean, maybe?"

"Well, I just remembered something," I say. "We're talking about the night Dora argued with Ransbleen. Dora's neighbor told me about that. And she also told me that Dora had beef with a coworker. The neighbor said the coworker turned out to be Dora's enemy. And the coworker threatened Dora."

"So, what are you thinking, sis?"

I glance at the cat. "I'm thinking that maybe Ransbleen didn't kill Dora. Maybe it was Marlo Green …"

# Chapter 39

"Okay, sis, what's the plan?" asks Callie, trotting around the sitting area as I finish the breakfast the staff delivered to me an hour ago.

"I'm getting dressed and going to Ransbleen's office," I say. "I'm going to tell him I want to donate to the Save the Bees charity and see if he'll take the check."

"But I thought you changed your mind about the crypt keeper," says Callie, jumping up onto the divan opposite me. "You think Marlo Green might have killed Dora."

Nodding, I pop a melon chunk into my mouth and chew it.

Yesterday, after I remembered my conversation with Dora's neighbor, the cat and I engaged in speculation, as well as applying the motive, means, and opportunity test to Marlo Green. She passed with flying colors, in my opinion.

Dora learned that Marlo was making the hypnotic honey spray and supplying it to her cousin, Ransbleen, so he could use it to con wealthy clients, which gives Marlo a motive to kill Dora. Marlo, as an employee of the medical center, had access to bee venom, which gives her means. And Marlo picked Dora up from the medical spa the night before she was found dead on the beach the following day. Marlo told the cops she dropped Dora off, then drove home, but I don't think that's true. I think it's entirely possible that Marlo injected Dora with bee venom, then dumped her body on the beach and covered it with dead bees.

"I do think Marlo could have killed Dora," I say. "But Ransbleen has a strong motive, as well. Nevertheless, I still don't have any hard evidence against either one of them. However, when Ransbleen deposits my donation check, I can follow the money and expose his fraud. Detective François should be persuaded to reopen the investigation, especially when I show him Dora's diary."

"Didn't she write things about malfeasance going on at the medical center?"

"Malfeasance?"

"Didn't you go to college?" asks the cat, licking her toe beans. "You should know what malfeasance means."

Giggling, I say, "I know what the word means. I think it's an interesting choice. But, yes, Dora did write about not trusting people and being threatened. I wish she'd used the real names of the culprits."

"Girl, she was probably afraid the diary might fall into the wrong hands."

I nod. "But obviously, Marlo and Ransbleen figured out Dora was on to them without finding the diary."

"And one of them got rid of her," says the cat.

"One of them being the man I'm going to talk to," I say, telling myself that my racing pulse has more to do with nervous excitement than apprehension.

"Speaking of that," says the cat. "Are you going to give him a bad check? Because you don't have the kind of money these other women are donating."

"No, but Vivian and Leo do," I say. "They deposited money into my account so I can write the check to Ransbleen's fake charity. I'm guessing he's going to cash the check or deposit it into an offshore account, instead of depositing it into the Save the Bees bank account."

"Girl, there is no Save the Bees bank account."

"I'm sure there isn't," I say. "If the charity was legit, there would be. Speaking of the fake charity, I need to get ready to talk to Ransbleen."

An hour later, dressed in a sky-blue sleeveless wrap dress, I venture out of my suite, with Callie in my arms, since she demanded to come along with me. Just in case Ransbleen tries anything funny with me. She promised, of course, to scratch his eyes right out of his head.

It's a lovely tropical morning, sunshine, blue skies, and a cool sea breeze, but I'm too nervous to enjoy the lovely weather.

"How do you think it's going to go, sis?" asks Callie.

Walking along the path to the administrative building, I shake my head. "I'm not sure. Just hope I don't mess up another sting."

"You could practice what you're going to say to him," suggests the feline.

"That's a good idea," I say, following the meandering path through the vibrant, lush vegetation. "I think I'll start by telling him that Felice DuFault told me about the charity and I thought it sounded like a worthwhile endeavor."

"Good idea to mention Felice," says the cat. "That gives you credibility."

"And then I'll tell him I want to donate," I say. "I'll say that bees are very important to our ecosystem and environment. You know, they pollinate the flowers that keep our island so beautiful."

"Sounds good," says the cat. "I'm sure he'll want to take your money."

"Let's hope so," I say, putting the cat on the ground as I walk up the steps toward the entrance doors of the administration building.

After entering, Callie and I walk along the cool, dim, wide hallways, heading to Ransbleen's office. Along the way, we encounter a few other staff members, who smile politely, but the place seems deserted.

Minutes later, we round the corner and walk down the corridor leading to Ransbleen's office.

My heart races along with my mounting anxiousness.

"Here's hoping things go well," I whisper to Callie as we reach the door.

"Girl, you got this," encourages the cat.

Nodding, I lift my hand to knock on the door.

But as I do, the force of my fist on the wood pushes the door back, and I realize it must have been open.

"What …" I whisper, peeking into Ransbleen's office.

"I'm getting a bad feeling, sis," says Callie, trotting into the office.

"A bad feeling?" I follow the Calico.

Callie scampers around behind Ransbleen's desk as I glance around the office, which appears empty.

"Girl, you're not going to like this …" Callie leaps onto the chair.

Worried, I take a deep breath and tip-toe behind the desk.

Gasping, I stumble backward, staring at Ransbleen Reiss's lifeless body.

# Chapter 40

Dropping to my knees next to Ransbleen's body, I press two fingers against his neck.

"Girl, what are you doing?" demands the cat.

"Checking for a pulse," I say.

"Sis, he's dead," says Callie.

"I know …" I say, frowning at the general manager's bluish lips and pale gray skin. "I wonder what happened to him?"

Callie says, "Doesn't seem to be shot or stabbed."

I stare at the cat. "You think someone killed him?"

"The thought crossed my mind," admits Callie. "But maybe he had a heart attack. Or a stroke."

"You could be right," I say. "Or …"

"Or?"

Sighing, I say, "Or maybe his cousin Marlo Green killed him."

"I thought you heard him threaten her," says the cat.

"I did," I say. "They were arguing about money. Marlo needed it to leave the island, but Ransbleen refused to give it to her unless she made more honey spray. She might have done it, then demanded money from him. And he might have reneged on their deal ... and she might have killed him."

"But how?" Callie asks, sniffing around Ransbleen's head. "I don't think she hit him with anything."

Sitting back on my heels, I open my cross-body purse. "I'm going to call Officer Cuetee and have him send the police. Then I'll tell Dr. Napier."

"Hurry up and do it, sis," instructs the cat. "This corpse is starting to smell like a crypt."

With shaking hands, I dial Officer Cuetee's number. When he picks up after three or four rings, I rush out, "Oh, thank goodness you picked up!"

"Sophie?" Officer Cuetee sounds concerned and confused. "What's going on? Are you okay?"

"Not really," I say. "Yes, I mean, I'm okay, but ... Ransbleen Reiss definitely is not okay."

"Ransbleen Reiss?"

"The general manager at the Bee Well Medical Center," I tell him. "He's ... dead."

"Dead?" echoes Officer Cuetee.

Glancing at Ransbleen's still form, I swallow. "Can you and Detective François come out to Bee Island? I think he might have been murdered."

"Okay, listen," says Officer Cuetee. "I'll round up a few other officers and we'll get there as soon as we can. In the meantime, notify the security team at the center, and ... wait, where are you?"

"Ransbleen's office," I say.

"Stay there until security comes, but try not to disturb anything," says Officer Cuetee. "When security gets there, they should close the office, cordon off the area, and make sure that everyone in the building is sent to a secure location until we can question everyone."

"Okay, got it," I say, my voice trembling.

"Don't worry, Soph," says Officer Cuetee. "We'll be there soon. The island is only thirty minutes from St. Mateo."

"Okay," I tell him. "See you soon."

"Is Officer Cuetee on his way?" asks Callie.

Nodding, I put my phone back in my purse. "He wants me to inform security, so that's—"

A door slams.

Startled, I gasp, jumping to my feet.

Marlo Green stands in front of the door.

"Oh, hi …" I say, my heart pounding. "I'm actually glad to see you …"

"Girl, why are you lying to that psycho?" asks Callie, jumping onto the desk.

Sneering, Marlo says, "Yeah, I doubt that."

"No, really," I say, hoping to convince her, wary of the malicious glint in her piercing gaze. "Mr. Reiss must have had a horrible medical event and … well, he's dead … and so—"

"It wasn't a horrible medical event," says Marlo. "It was bee venom."

I swallow. "Bee venom?"

"She killed him with bee venom, too?" asks the cat.

"Apparently," I whisper to the cat out of the side of my mouth.

"That's so odd," I say to Marlo. "I wonder how he died from bee venom."

"I injected it into him," admits Marlo, smirking. "But I suspect you know that. Just like you know that I killed Dora Butler."

Shaking my head, I say, "What? You killed Dora—"

"Don't pretend you don't know, okay?"

My shoulder slumping, I whisper to Callie, "She's on to me."

Marlo releases a slow exhale. "I told Ransbleen you would be a problem, but my stupid cousin didn't believe me. Not even when I showed him your press pass, proving that you're a reporter from the *Palmchat Gazette* and not some wealthy West Indian heiress."

So that's why she took my press pass, I think, then ask, "And what did Ransbleen say when you told him who I really am?"

Scoffing, Marlo says, "He didn't care, even though I told him you were investigating Dora Butler's death. How did he put it? The fact that Dora was found dead on the beach had nothing to do with him."

"But it had everything to do with you," I say.

Marlo shrugs. "Ransbleen said it wasn't his problem. He didn't tell me to kill Dora. But he benefited from her death. Dora found out he was scamming the medical center's rich clients."

"With the hypnotizing spray," I say. "He tricked the clients into donating to his fake charity."

"So you figured that out, too," says Marlo, still blocking the door. "Just like Dora did. And, I suppose, you're planning to go to the police, like Dora was … before I stopped her."

"I don't understand," I say. "I thought Dora was your friend."

"Friendly coworker," clarifies Marlo. "Until she caught me stealing bee hives."

"I don't understand," I say. "Why would you—"

"Why do you think?" asks Marlo. "These wrinkled old rich biddies have more money than sense. It's not like they even missed what they donated."

"And they didn't remember why they donated, either," I say. "Because of the honey spray you created."

Scoffing, Marlo says, "Those decrepit crones are obsessed with youth and beauty. The only thing they want to remember is when their skin cells still had enough collagen to keep their jowls from sagging."

Angered by her hatefulness, I say, "Maybe so, but that's still no reason to steal from them."

"You sound like Dora," Marlo says. "So self-righteous. She was a nurse wasting her time for half of what she was worth. I offered to give her a cut of the money, but she refused. She insisted on telling Napier, and the cops."

"What happened the night you killed her?"

"That's a good question, sis," says Callie. "A better question is, how are we going to get out of here?"

"I'm keeping her talking so I can think," I whisper from the side of my mouth again.

"I think I should scratch her eyes out," says the cat.

Marlo says, "Ransbleen went to Dora's house to pay her off. They argued, but Ransbleen was able to convince her to take the cash and keep her mouth shut. So they went to the day spa. Ransbleen gave her five thousand dollars. Then he took a ferry back to Bee Island. After he left, Dora called me, telling me she wanted to talk and that she needed a ride home. So, I drove to the day spa to pick her up."

"And what did you talk about?"

"Believe it or not, but Dora offered to give me the five thousand dollars if I would go with her to the cops to snitch on Ransbleen," says Marlo, shaking her head. "She tried to convince me that I could negotiate some type of immunity in exchange for giving the police information to arrest Ransbleen."

"What did you say?"

"I turned her down," Marlo says. "My cousin and I had a good thing going, fleecing these old broads. Then she told me she had no choice but to go to the police."

"So you had no choice but to kill her?" I ask.

Marlo gives me a ghoulish smile that reminds me of her cousin. "Just like I have no choice but to kill you …"

# Chapter 41

"Actually, I don't think killing me is the only choice you have," I tell Marlo, my heart slamming as I struggle to think my way out of this disastrous situation.

"Girl, she threatened to kill you?" asks Callie, hissing at Marlo. "Okay, time for me to scratch her eyes out. Good thing I've been sharpening my claws on these palm trees around the property."

"What's the other choice you think I have?" asks Marlo, removing something from the deep pocket of her cleaning smock.

A syringe needle.

Swallowing my fear, I say, "You can … take the money I was going to donate to your cousin's charity."

Holding the syringe between her fingers like a cigarette, Marlo frowns. "Did you forget that I know you're not a West Indian heiress? You don't have the kind of money Ransbleen scammed from these old biddies."

"You're right, I don't," I admit. "But my boss does. His name is Leo Bronson. He owns the *Palmchat Gazette,* and his parents are billionaires. He'll pay you whatever you want. Let me call him."

"You think I'm stupid?" asks Marlo, scowling. "You think I believe your employer is going to give up millions of dollars for you? Because that's my price. A million dollars."

"A million dollars is no big deal to Leo," I say. "And he will pay to keep me alive."

"Girl, she wants a million dollars?" asks Callie, sounding astonished. "She needs her eyes scratched out for that ridiculous audacity!"

"Maybe he will pay to keep you alive," says Marlo. "But ... will you really call him? Or, will you call the cops?"

"I promise," I say, a plan taking shape in my mind. "I won't call the cops. I'll take my phone out of my purse, put it on the desk, and you can call him. I'll recite the number to you."

Eyes narrowed, Marlo stares at me. "What if I want something in addition to the money?"

"Like what?"

Marlo says, "I need to get off this island. Can he arrange that? And get me new identification? I need to disappear."

Nodding, I say, "I know he can. His family has lots of contacts. Rich people are good at making things happen ... and staying quiet about it."

Marlo takes a deep breath, her gaze contemplative.

"What's going on, sis?" asks the cat.

Whispering, I say, "She needs help getting off the island ..."

"You know what else I need?" asks Marlo. "Someone to take the blame for Dora's murder, so it's not traced back to me."

"Well, you told the cops Ida killed Dora," I say.

"Yeah, but she didn't work as a suspect," says Marlo.

"So you tried to frame Ida?"

Shrugging, Marlo says, "It worked when I framed her before. I was able to convince Napier and Dr. Jones that she was stealing bee hives and got her fired. Even Dora believed it … until she didn't and realized I had stolen the hives."

Realizing Dora probably did believe that Ida, *worker bee #4*, was guilty before she learned the truth about Marlo, I ask, "How did Dora find out you were stealing hives?"

"The old-fashioned way," says Marlo, giving me another grim smile, reminiscent of her cousin. "She caught me red-handed."

Circling our conversation back to Ida, I say, "So, obviously, you weren't able to frame Ida a second time."

"I didn't realize that she went back to Australia after she was fired," says Marlo. "There was no way she could have killed Dora, which is a shame. I gave her a good motive when I told the cops Dora was afraid of her."

"Which wasn't true."

"Anyway, now you understand why I need a new scapegoat."

"I'm sure Leo can help with that, too," I say.

Marlo says, "Okay … give me your phone."

Thinking of my plan, which I just came up with and which is rather risky, I unzip my crossbody purse. But instead of reaching inside of it, I pivot toward the bookshelf, grab one of the books then turn and throw it at Marlo.

Cursing, Marlo ducks.

"Good idea, girl!" says Callie.

"You liar!" Marlo shouts, stomping toward the desk.

I grab another book, then toss it toward her, but Marlo bobs then weaves before continuing her approach.

"You gotta throw another book!" shouts Callie.

Pulling another book from the shelf, I turn and throw it, but my aim is off. Marlo avoids getting hit and instead lunges toward the desk.

"Girl, let's get out of here!" Callie says. "You opened the secret door!"

"What?" Confused, I face the wall between the bookshelves.

But it isn't there …

The narrow path through the thick, jungle vegetation stretches ahead of us. Grabbing Callie, I take off, glancing over my shoulder in time to see Marlo scramble over the desk and race after us …

# Chapter 42

"Put me down girl!" commands Callie as I run down the path.

"Are you sure?" I ask, huffing and puffing, struggling to breathe beneath the relentless, scorching sun. Despite the sea breeze, the humidity is higher today, making the air sticky and oppressive.

"You'll run faster if you don't have to carry me," the cat says.

"But I don't want anything to happen to you!" I tell Callie, pushing aside leaves and bushes that smack me in the face.

"Girl, I've got panther and cheetah in my DNA," says Callie. "I can get away from anything that tries to chase me. Now put me down! I have an idea …"

"What is it?"

"Lead the psycho to the shack," says Callie. "I'll take it from there."

Though I'm worried, wondering what the cat has planned, I nevertheless slow to a running jog and lean over, allowing her to jump from my arms. As she scampers into the underbrush, my heart sinks. The thought of something bad happening to Callie would break my heart, but she's a fierce feline. I have to believe that whatever plan she's cooked up might work.

If I play my part …

I need to lead Marlo to the shack.

Glancing over my shoulder, fresh panic explodes within me.

Marlo is close behind, maybe ten feet away, snarling and cursing and shouting, obviously determined to catch up with me and inject a lethal dose of bee venom into my veins. Increasing my pace, I take off, stumbling and slipping on the dirt and gravel. But I'm determined not to fall. Focused on getting to the shack.

And worried about the cat.

What could she have planned?

Hopefully nothing that might get her hurt. Or worse. The thought of something bad happening to Callie makes my stomach twist. Makes me wish I had a more accurate aim. If only I had connected when I'd thrown the book at Marlo Green. Not that I would have knocked her out, but I could have disoriented her enough to get past her and out of Ransbleen's office.

I'd rather be running through the halls of the administration building instead of through the jungle, but—

Something rakes the back of my arm.

Screaming, I look behind me.

Marlo is on my heels, trying to grab me. Facing her, marshaling every ounce of anger I can muster, I make a fist and punch her in the face. My knuckles crash against her cheekbone, which seems to hurt both of us.

Eyes wide with shock, Marlo cries out, holding her jaw.

"Ow!" I wince, shaking my hand as I take off again, running faster than ever, not bothering to look back, knowing that Marlo is right behind me as I follow the trail. But it's okay because the shack is in sight. About fifteen feet ahead.

Grunting, I dash toward the opening, my feet skittering as I head into the dilapidated structure. Scrambling to a stop, right before I barrel into several wall-mounted wooden shelves housing a half dozen cans of honey spray, I pivot to face Marlo.

Holding the needle in the air like a knife, Marlo rushes toward me, and—

Out of nowhere, Callie leaps at Marlo, sinking her claws into the woman's face. Screaming, Marlo drops the needle, spinning and jerking, desperately trying to get the Calico to loosen her hold.

"Get off me!" Marlo howls, drunkenly side-stepping, swaying to and fro as she clutches Callie, trying to pull the cat off her—which I know, from experience, is not going to work. When Callie grabs hold of you, she doesn't let go.

"Callie!" I scream. "Be careful!"

"Girl, get one of those honey sprays!" The cat instructs.

"Okay!" I turn, rush to the shelves, and grab a can. "I got it!"

"I'm going to let go of her," says Callie, hissing in Marlo's face. "When I do, you spray her!"

"Are you sure that's going to work?" I ask the cat, feinting left and right, away from Marlo as she whirls around like a disoriented spinning top. "The spray is not poison!"

"No, but it's hypnotic!" says the cat. "You can make her obey you!"

Understanding the cat's plan, I say, "Gotcha! Let her go!"

Seconds later, Callie leaps away from Marlo, who, obviously dizzy and confused, falls to her knees. Springing into action, I press the nozzle on the can and give her a full face of the honey spray.

"No!" Marlo screams, desperately wiping her face, smearing the honey-smelling spray all over her skin.

"Now tell her to sit down and stay quiet!" says Callie, walking toward me.

"I've got a better idea," I say as Marlo slumps onto her side, babbling incoherently. "The police will be here soon, Marlo. When they arrive, I'm going to clap my hands three times … and then you will confess all your crimes."

"There's something I don't understand," says Officer Cuetee, beckoning me around to the side of the shack as the deputies who showed up with him thirty minutes ago process the scene.

Marlo Green sits on the ground, handcuffed, giving a statement to one of the senior officers.

"What's that?" I ask, reaching down to pick up Callie.

"Don't get used to this, girl," warns the cat as she snuggles in my arms. "I'm only letting you hold me because I ran a long way and I deserve the rest."

"Right," I say, giving her a quick head scritch.

Officer Cuetee frowns. "Right about what?"

"Oh, um …" I clear my throat. "What was it that you don't understand?"

Giving me a look of amused suspicion, Officer Cuetee says, "Why did Marlo Green start confessing to killing Dora Butler and Ransbleen Reiss?"

"Well," I hedge, recalling the moment when the cops came running toward the shed and I clapped my hands three times. "It's kind of complicated. But, basically, Marlo and Ransbleen had a scam going where they used a hypnotic spray to trick rich clients into donating to a fake charity."

"Are you serious?"

"Marlo is probably telling the officer herself," I say. "You saw those cans on the shelf?"

Nodding, Officer Cuetee says, "That was the hypnotic spray?"

"It smells like honey," I say, giving the cat another pet as she slowly closes her eyes. "Marlo Green was a housekeeper here at the medical center. She would spray it in the rooms of the clients they were going to fleece. And then Ransbleen sprayed it on the clients again and used it to hypnotize them."

"That's crazy," says Officer Cuetee, shaking his head.

"But it works," I say. "That's why Marlo started confessing. I told her to come clean when I clapped my hands three times."

"Well, we'll have the CSI lab analyze the cans of spray," says Officer Cuetee.

"You'll probably want to search Marlo's residence," I say. "She's probably got stolen bee hives and a stockpile of bee venom. That's how she killed Dora and Ransbleen."

Smiling, Officer Cuetee says, "And you found all that out."

"Yeah," I say, smiling back at him. "I actually did."

"You know what that means right?"

Confused, I say, "Um … that I'm well on my way to becoming the world's best investigative reporter."

"Maybe," he says. "But, for sure, you pulled off your first successful sting operation."

"Oh my gosh!" I say, laughing. "You're right. This is my first successful sting!"

"And you couldn't have done it without me, sis," says Callie, yawning.

"No, I couldn't have," I whisper, nuzzling the cat. "You and I did it together …"

# Epilogue

"Hey, girl, hey ..." says Callie as I walk toward my JEEP, waving at her.

It's an overcast, humid day, threatening rain, but I've still got my head in the clouds. I've been floating on Cloud Nine all week since my story about Dora Butler's death came out.

As soon as it was posted to the paper's website and social media pages, it began to trend.

***Bee Venom Deaths Linked to Fake Charity Scam*** is my most successful story to date, and so far has brought in additional subscribers and followers. Advertising dollars will follow, which Leo is happy about. Vivian is proud of my accomplishments, and even Marty grudgingly admitted that the article was very informative, engaging, and in-depth. He stopped short of announcing that I do, indeed, have "it", but he's more confident that I'll do a good job if he sends me out to cover more crime stories.

"What's going on?" I ask the cat, who I've seen off and on since we got back from Bee Island. After spending so much time together, Callie declared she needed space, but she wouldn't be gone for long. I respect her need for independence, even though I've missed her.

"How's the bee venom story doing?" Callie asks.

"Great," I say. "People are interested and invested. And I meant to tell you … I found out some other things about Marlo Green."

"Like what?" the cat asks, licking her fur.

"First of all, Marlo told the police that on the night she picked Dora up from the day spa," I say. "She called a cab, told the driver to drop her off two blocks from Dora's street, then walked the rest of the way to Dora's house."

"So there would be no record of her going back to Dora's that night," concludes the cat.

"Right," I say. "She pretended that she wanted to go to the cops and snitch on her cousin, Ransbleen. When Dora turned her back, Marlo stabbed her in the neck with the bee venom. Then she put Dora's body in the back of Dora's car, drove to the beach, and left her body there."

"What about the dead bees?"

"Marlo actually drove back to her house, in Dora's car, and got a bag of dead bees that she'd previously killed, and covered Dora's body with them," I say.

"Did she tell the cops why she did that?"

"Marlo claimed she couldn't remember."

"Effects of the spray?" asks the cat.

"Possibly," I say. "And speaking of the spray, it turns out Marlo was a hypno-chemist."

"A hypno-chemist?" The cat stares at me. "Girl, what is that?"

"Apparently, a hypno-chemist uses chemical compounds to aid in hypnosis," I say. "But she lost her license after she was accused of hypnotizing patients into signing over their life savings to them."

"So, she wasn't new to scamming, she was true to it," surmises the Calico.

Nodding, I say, "She cooked up the scheme with her cousin Ransbleen, who was actually a disgraced former doctor."

"The crypt keeper was a doctor?" asks the cat.

"Hard to believe, I know," I say, recalling my research. "I'm thinking he must have been the doctor Dora referred to in her diary."

"Yeah, Dr. Frankenstein," says the cat.

"And remember I told you that Mrs. DuFault would get a phone call and hear a buzzing sound?"

Bobbing her head, the cat says, "What was that about?"

"It was a hypnotic suggestion," I say. "Marlo confessed that when the clients were under the hypnotic spell, Ransbleen told them that when they got a call and heard bees buzzing, they were to donate to the charity."

"Girl, that is diabolical," says the cat.

"You were right in comparing Ransbleen to Frankenstein," I say. "He was an absolute monster. And Marlo was his Igor."

"Sis, you do know that in the original story, there is no Igor, right?" asks the cat.

"Oh, um ..."

My cell phone pings. Relieved, because I totally didn't know that information about the Igor character, I remove my phone from my purse.

"Who is that?" asks the cat.

Staring at my phone, I say, "Officer Cuetee. He wants me to call him."

"Well, call him, girl," says the cat. "Maybe he wants to ask you out."

Trying not to blush, I glance at Callie. "You think so?"

"You know he likes you," the Calico says.

Biting my lip, I sigh, then dial Officer Cuetee's number. When he answers after two rings, I say, "Hey, it's Sophie ..."

"Hey, I don't have much time, but I thought you'd want to know this ..."

Curious, I ask, "What?"

"Is he asking you out?" asks the cat. "Tell him to take you to a fancy seafood restaurant so I can tag along and get fresh tuna."

I smile and shake my head at the cat as Officer Cuetee says, "I got some information about the CCTV across from the *Palmchat Gazette* building ... "

"Oh ..." I say, shocked. When I asked Officer Cuetee for help with the CCTV, I don't think I expected him to find anything. But, if he has, I need to know if it might be a clue to Callie's past.

"Uh oh," says the cat. "I guess he's not asking you out."

"Not exactly," I whisper to the feline.

"Unfortunately, there's something disturbing on the video," says Officer Cuetee. "You definitely need to see it."

# Also by Rachel Woods

**SASSY SARCASTIC CAT COZY MYSTERIES**

Sophie Carter, a struggling reporter for the *Palmchat Gazette*, teams up with a sassy talking Calico cat to solve crimes as she strives to become an influential investigative reporter

A SLY AND SINISTER TAIL

A COLD AND CUNNING TAIL

A FOUL AND FEARSOME TAIL

A DARK AND DEVIOUS TAIL

**REPORTER ROLAND BEAN COZY MYSTERIES**

Roland "Beanie" Bean, husband and loving father, finds himself the unwitting participant in solving crimes as he seeks to make a name for himself as a reporter for the *Palmchat Gazette*.

HAPPY BIRTHDAY MURDER

EASTER EGG HUNT MURDER

MERRY CHRISTMAS MURDER

TRICK OR TREAT MURDER

GOBBLE GOBBLE MURDER

HAPPY 4TH OF JULY MURDER

SUMMER VACATION MURDER

HAPPY NEW YEAR MURDER

**PALMCHAT ISLANDS MYSTERIES**

Married journalists, Vivian and Leo, manage the island newspaper while solving crimes as they chase leads for their next story.

UNTIL DEATH DO US PART

NO ONE WILL FIND YOU

YOU WILL DIE FOR THIS

DON'T MAKE ME HURT YOU

THE PALMCHAT ISLANDS MYSTERIES BOX SET: BOOKS 1 - 4

## RUTHLESS REVENGE ROMANCE SERIES

Gripping romantic suspense series with steamy romance, unpredictable plot twists and devastating consequences of deceit.

HER DEADLY MISTAKE

HER DEADLY DECEPTION

HER DEADLY THREAT

HER DEADLY BETRAYAL

## MURDER IN PARADISE SERIES

A series of stand-alone women sleuth mysteries with murder, mayhem and a dash of romance, set against the backdrop of turquoise waters and swaying palm trees of the fictional Palmchat Islands.

THE UNWORTHY WIFE

THE SILENT ENEMY

THE PERFECT LIAR

# About the Author

Rachel Woods studied journalism and graduated from the University of Houston where she published articles in the Daily Cougar. She is a legal assistant by day and a freelance writer and blogger with a penchant for melodrama by night. Many of her stories take place on the islands, which she has visited around the world. Rachel resides in Houston, Texas with her three sock monkeys.

*For more information:*
www.therachelwoods.com
rachel@therachelwoods.com

# About the Publisher

**BONZAIMOON BOOKS**

BonzaiMoon Books is a family-run, artisanal publishing company created in the summer of 2014. We publish works of fiction in various genres. Our passion and focus is working with authors who write the books you want to read, and giving those authors the opportunity to have more direct input in the publishing of their work.

*For more information:*
www.bonzaimoonbooks.com
info@bonzaimoonbooks.com